Nize
The Making of a Champion

by Esther Myles

SlapDash Publishing, LLC
Carolina Beach, North Carolina

LIBRARY OF CONGRESS
CONTROL NUMBER: **2008930203**
Esther Myles
Nize – The Making of a Champion
Carolina Beach, N.C., SlapDash Publishing, LLC.
180 pp.

Published by:

slapdash • publishing LLC

311 Florida Avenue, Carolina Beach, NC 28428
910.232.0604 • info@carolinabeach.net
www.carolinabeach.net

International Standard Book Number:
978-0-9792431-3-4

First Printing
July 2008

 Dedicated to the memory of my parents

Anson and Hillery N. Babson

Contents

Prologue

The events portrayed in the in the book, "Nize", take place in the 1940's, 50's and 60's.

In 1939, the United States emerged from ten years of the greatest financial depression ever experienced in western memory. The horrific events of "Black Friday", when the stock market collapsed in 1929, were followed some four years later, with the failure of the United States banking system. President Herbert Hoover stumbled from his bed on a chilly and gray dawn on March 4, 1933, his last official day as President, to this disastrous news. The event marked the final defeat of his infamous term of office. "We are at the end of our rope and there is nothing more we can do." he mournfully announced. His words echoed the spirit of the nation, and the spiraling descent of the country's fortunes under his leadership.

Some 13 to 15 million people found themselves unemployed. Another 30 million of their dependents wondered where they would get their next meal. Those who were employed, saw hourly wages drop 60% and white collar salaries drop 40%. Homeless, starving and financially ruined, many Americans had given up hope for themselves, their families, and their country.

Nize would have been born at the end of this period, as the nation began to pull itself into better times, only to be plunged again, in 1941, into World War II. The "war effort" and the dynamic leadership of President Franklin D. Roosevelt, with his radio "fireside chats" and his famous inaugural statement, "We have nothing to fear but fear itself!", galvanized the nation. His words propelled America into the "golden" years of the fifties and sixties, when anything seemed possible.

Lessons of frugality, thankfulness and willingness to work hard for every dollar, were the foundation of this new era in America. A hopeful and expanding economy launched some of America's greatest achievements. These culminated, in 1969, when Neil Armstrong, the first person to step onto the moon's surface, exclaimed, "One small step for man, one giant leap for mankind!"

Inspirational leadership, begun under Roosevelt, continued in the 60's with the inspiring example and words of Martin Luther King's, "I Have a Dream" speech. President John F. Kennedy started the "Peace Corp" program and in his 1961 inaugural statement he said these unforgettable words in his address to America, "Ask not what your country can do for you; ask what you can do for your country."

The foundation of America's rise to greatness were the millions of hardworking Americans, like Nize's parents, who by sheer will power, backbreaking work, frugality, humor, deep spiritual faith, indomitable spirit and strict moral code, raised a generation who rose to new and wonderful levels of achievement, giving America once more the power to believe in the "American Dream" of independence, success and happiness.

Chapter One

Ferry Ride

Nize walked to the front of the large ferry as it slowly and steadily made its journey northward on the Cape Fear River toward Pleasure Island and into the most beautiful sunset she had ever seen. She saw a large seagull fly by and land in the rippling water brightened by the light from the sunset's reflection. Her eyes rested there for a long time, and then her thoughts went back to a time twenty-one years ago to another river with dark rippling water.

She thought about the banks of the peaceful Waccamaw River on a Sunday morning years before. She was thirteen years old and anxiously waiting in line by the river to be baptized. She watched Preacher Harmony as he stood waist deep in the water wearing his Sunday suit and tie. He gently submerged each new convert in the water as if he was a famous dancer dipping a beautiful lady in waltz and whispering in her ear, "Your life will be changed; you will have a friend forever; he will never forsake you, and he will love you unconditionally."

Two days earlier, Nize's mother had said to her, "You will accompany me to our church's revival tonight." Nize's father, who was not much for going to church since he was usually tired from long days engaged in farm labor, nodded his head in approval. Encouraging her, he said, "That's the best place a young lady can go." After the hard years of the Depression that the family had survived, Nize's parents knew they had FDR's New Deal and their own faith in God to thank. Though life had been difficult for everyone, they had made it through that and then the war years, and their faith was stronger because of it.

Nize's mother had made her a new turquoise dress the day before. Nize was happy the dress had a matching jacket so that it could be worn to cover up a ripe, swollen pimple on her shoulder. At age thirteen, it was obvious Nize was quickly becoming a young woman. Nize's thick, mink-like hair accented her sun-tanned face. Nize's mother knew that a new dress would make it easier for her to walk into church that evening. Nize and her friends from school didn't think going to church was the coolest thing to do. The idea of the preacher screaming about "hell and damnation" made Nize wish she could just run from the large but seemingly confining front door of the church. God forbid that any of her friends should see her tonight, even if she was wearing a new sundress.

Deacon King stepped up to the pulpit and announced to the faithful that Reverend Harmony would be conducting the revival services. Deacon King then told all gathered that the Reverend had traveled quite a distance to be there.

Reverend Harmony stood up behind the pulpit and spoke to the large congregation. Nize quickly lifted up her eyes, which had been focused on a spot on the worn wooden floor. This voice was so gentle, soft, and with a strange charisma that was different somehow and quickly got her complete attention. It was not only the tone of the voice, but what he was saying seemed so right. Reverend Harmony spoke of God's love with so much passion, gentleness, humility, and peace that Nize slowly began to feel a love she had yet to feel. Even though she loved her family, this love was different. Perhaps it was love on a higher plane. Reverend Harmony spoke long enough to explain in simple terms how a person could come to have this love forever.

Shortly after, Nize and her mother rose from their pews to join the congregation in singing the invitational hymn. Nize then bravely walked down the church's aisle to commit her life to God. Nize was met by the outstretched arms of Reverend Harmony. Nize felt the church's love and acceptance all around her, and as someone gave her a big hug, she felt the swollen pimple on her shoulder pop. She felt no pain or embarrassment, only happiness and the peace of knowing she would have a friend with her, forever. In the many years that followed, there would be so many times Nize would think about Reverend Harmony's words.

Today was certainly no exception. As she watched the ferry part the waters of the Cape Fear River on its journey north, she saw the seagull resting in the sunset-colored water lift its wings and take flight. She heard the Reverend's words from so long ago echoing in her head. Nize needed comfort today, fearing she had lost someone who was irreplaceable.

Chapter Two

Family

Family was important to Nize's parents, in fact it was their greatest possession. Having grown up as a preacher's daughter, Nize's mama was as stern as she was hard working. She believed, "Spare not the rod, lest you spoil the child." Only Nize's papa could lighten her mood and make her laugh when she was down. Papa was a very happy man with a big heart full of love. He and his only daughter had developed a strong bond. Both father and daughter had good looks. Nize's mother sometimes referred to them as "two peas in a pod." Nize's only brother, Roger, was more like their mother. He worked hard and was obedient. It was obvious to everyone that he was Mama's favorite. Mama could relate to him a little more; they were very close.

Papa had married Mama with only five dollars in his pocket. He was a loving husband and a determined farmer. He cleared the land on their first farm by hand. The only help he received was from a mule and his devoted wife, who worked long hours by his side. There was always plenty of laughter and happiness in Nize's childhood home, except when someone neglected to do their chores. When this happened, the guilty person would receive a stern lecture about the virtues of hard work. This was usually enough to set them straight.

Secretly, Nize longed for a more colorful and exciting life. One with lots of pretty things and interesting people. Most of Nize's surroundings were simple because all of the family's extra money was saved to buy more land for the farm. More land meant more crops and income, but it meant more work as well.

However, on one spring afternoon, after the long walk home from school, Nize got the surprise of her young life. Even though she was tired, Nize noticed something sitting on top of her mother's sewing machine when she walked through the front door. It was the most beautiful and colorful thing she had ever seen: Anna, Nize's old doll, but transformed now in a lovely new hot pink dress adorned with ribbons, and a bonnet to match. Nize stood there in the front room, drinking in the outfit's beauty as she carefully reached for the doll. Even with all her other chores, Mama had made time to do this for Nize.

Mama was an extraordinary person who would rise early in the morning and work side by side with Papa, all the while managing to cook the best meals around. Visitors were always welcome to share, and her house was always immaculate. She was the wise person that the community looked to for advice in times of trouble and the person who cared for the sick and elderly neighbors and relatives. When needed, she counseled Papa on business, kept the paperwork for the farm, and took care of church duties. But she always had time to stop in her chores and help Nize with the many beauty projects Nize dreamed up. Mama knew she loved pretty things and managed to help cultivate this love in the middle of her farm life. In another time and life Nize's mama would have been considered "a grand lady" who always wore a strand of pearls and her wedding band. In the world Nize grew up in, Mama was a giant, with the soul and wisdom of a saint.

At the same time, Mama demanded perfection of herself and all around her. Nize and her brother learned many lessons from her throughout their childhood. They knew to be honest, punctual, thrifty, and industrious in all they did, as mistakes and slack efforts were promptly dealt with by Mama. Holding her old doll in its new clothes, though, Nize knew that the soft and kind part of her mother was just as much a part of her as the stern disciplinarian. Nize was grateful for both.

Chapter Three

The Makeover

Papa was a very creative person who especially liked to make things for his children with his hands. Whenever he had a little extra money and a little extra time, he would craft toys for them.

One fall, Papa decided his chores on the farm would just have to wait until he completed a project he had been planning for some time. It began when he came home one day with two wagon wheels, a hammer, nails, boards, and his saw. He soon presented his two children with a sturdy cart he had painted bright red. Nize and Roger were beside themselves. They could hardly wait to play with the new toy their Papa had made for them.

But who will pull the cart?" they wondered. A few days later, Papa came home with a large white goat in the back of his old red truck. The goat had no horns, but he did have a very hard head where there had once been horns. Nize soon learned to respect the white goat's hard head. Billy, the name Nize and her brother had given the goat, quickly took a dislike to Nize and would chase her anytime she came into view. Once she was able to get into the cart, though, her brother would hook the goat to the front and quickly hop in beside her. Nize and Roger, with his hands held tightly on the reins, sat on the cart with Billy happily trotting down the road. It was a sight to see.

The children enjoyed many days with Billy pulling the cart. Sometimes they helped Papa by loading vegetables from the garden in the cart and delivering them to Mama as she canned food for the winter. Through it all, Nize kept thinking, "I must make Billy like me, so I don't have to run every time I'm near him."

Nize considered how she could win the goat over. Her friends always liked it when she did makeovers on them. Their parents would hardly recognize them after one of Nize's transforming makeovers. Clean clothes, new hairstyles, a little make-up, and a smile on their face always changed a person dramatically. Nize thought maybe Billy would like one too.

One day, after her brother had temporarily tied Billy to the post, she quickly returned with a box of her mother's make-up. Soon Billy's huge goat lips were a vivid shade of bright red, the fur on his face was pink with rouge, and his long eyelashes seemed even longer after a couple of coats of black mascara. "A masterpiece," Nize thought. "But how can Billy appreciate his new look if he can't see himself?" As Nize held her mother's hand mirror in front of his face, Billy saw an unfamiliar goat in the mirror. His competitive male goat instinct turned into anger as he saw the odd reflection. He began to stomp and pull at the rope holding him. Soon his brute strength broke the rope, and the mirror landed on the ground. With the strange reflection gone, Nize once again became the target of Billy's anger. Aided by her skinny legs, Nize made a beeline for the porch with the goat in hot pursuit. She skipped two steps as she ran to the front door and slammed it in Billy's glamorous face, just in time to stop his hard head from knocking her through the doorway. As she put a chair against the door, she could feel her heart beating rapidly through her blouse. Billy continued to pound on the door for what seemed like an eternity. The family was working out in the fields, so Nize was alone — barricaded in her house with a lipstick-wearing, ticked off goat at her front door. Eventually, she heard the "clop, clop, clop" of Billy's feet as he gave up and walked off the porch.

Nize realized she was never going to be Billy's favorite playmate, so she developed a strategy out of pure desperation. Having observed that Billy enjoyed playing with one of her mother's silk stockings he had found in the trash, she never went outside without one in her pocket. A silk stocking waved in front of Billy was the one thing he preferred to chasing her.

When the children played cowboys, Nize was always the local sheriff. She was a natural leader and well-respected by others. She was good at winning games or starting new activities with her friends. But, Billy — well, that was another story. Nize was smart enough to wave the white flag (or silk stocking) when it became necessary.

Chapter Four

The Local Sheriff

Some folks in the neighborhood who knew about the secret productions behind Papa's old barn affectionately called Nize "the local sheriff." She and her brother were privileged to be able to listen to Papa's tall wooden radio during the daylight hours. But at dusk, when the neighborhood men had finished their work in the fields, they would gather close to the old radio and listen to the latest news from the war. Since there was no television in the house and there was rarely any extra money for going to the movies, the children oftentimes had to be creative and make their own entertainment.

The "movie theatre" became Nize and her brother's joint venture after they nailed one of Mama's white bed sheets to two tall poles and lifted it behind Papa's old barn. Thus a movie screen was born. Cinder blocks were used to provide simple seating. All that was needed was a cast, and since the theatre was constructed on her family's land, Nize usually got the lead part. She would be the princess, the cowboy, or the local sheriff, as other actors joined her with their horses made of old garden stakes. They would gallop in front of the large bed sheet until all the bad guys were chased out of town. Of course, justice always prevailed when Nize locked all the undesirables up in the local jail.

Most of the neighborhood children came to watch anytime there was a production, but some adults, out of curiosity, wanted to see what the young folks were up to. Occasionally they would peek behind the old barn, and often the drama unfolding would draw them in until they found themselves perched on cinder blocks alongside the children, waiting to see what would happen to the villains.

Since then, many neighbors addressed Nize as "the local sheriff" when they needed a good laugh. That was alright with Nize as she continued to entertain the children for a long time in the theatre she and her brother had constructed.

Chapter Five

Sweet Sixteen

The store-bought dress was made of soft taffeta. The color was fuchsia pink with layers of ruffles from the dress's waist down to the ankle length hem. When Nize tried it on and swirled around, the skirt stood out like a large, open umbrella. She had never felt this pretty before.

Nize's closest friend, Mattie, was turning sixteen the same week. A big party for both of them was set for Saturday night at Mattie's house. Classmates from school were invited as well as a few of Mattie's older brother's friends, who were visiting from college, including a Casanova football star that was known as the handsomest man in town. "Roger will pick you up at ten o'clock sharp," Mama shouted, as Nize left for the party.

There were festive decorations all around the house, and a large cake with six-teen candles was already lit and waiting to be blown out when Nize arrived for the party. Nize drew in a quick breath at her side of the cake and, along with Mattie, blew as hard as she could. Just as she was making a wish, the sound of a car's engine made her open her eyes. She saw, through the window, a baby blue Studebaker pulling into the driveway.

Nize saw a young man emerging from the car and slowly walking up the porch stairs and into the living room. He was immaculately dressed with blond hair combed to the side and white buck shoes clean as a whistle. Nize couldn't take her eyes off the blond-haired young man. She realized that she was staring and tried to focus her gaze on the other side of the room before he noticed. This was as hard to do as going to the dentist. The young man was different from the boys at Nize's school, though she couldn't say exactly why.

While the party-goers chatted and sipped punch, Nize watched the man chat with Mattie's older brother for a while before turning and swaggering onto the front porch. Within minutes, Nize had a strong urge for some fresh air. She softly closed the front door behind her as she stepped out onto the porch, and she timidly walked toward the swing where he was sitting, trying to think of something to say.

The young man's gaze started at the top of Nize's head and slowly moved all the way down to her feet, then back up to her eyes, where they focused as he rose and walked toward her. Stopping only inches away, the young man bent his head and lightly kissed Nize on the lips. She closed her eyes for one second, experiencing the odd sensation of her first kiss, and thinking of the wish she had just made as she blew out her birthday candles.

Suddenly, instinct took over and the palm of Nize's right hand sharply met the side of the blond-haired man's face. Jumping back, he turned quickly and walked towards his car, rubbing his wounded cheek. He smiled at her over the top of the Studebaker before getting in, revving the engine, and speeding down the driveway.

Nize just stood there, stunned. It had all happened so quickly. She had done exactly what her mother had always told her to do, hadn't she? "Make a man respect you and you can respect yourself." So, if this was the right thing for a young lady to do, why did she feel so lousy? She watched as he drove away, and after a few minutes she went back inside to open the presents from her friends and family. Other than some left over stinging in her hand, her Sweet Sixteen had been a good one. She felt like something had changed during the night, though running her fingers lightly over her lips, she couldn't figure out just what.

Chapter Six

Speed

Nize was still sad and confused the next morning, but not for long. She heard an unfamiliar car horn blasting outside, and there was a strong, loud knock on the front door. Nize ran to see who was there and when she opened the door, there stood Mattie with a silly grin on her face. Mattie pointed, and there, parked in the driveway, was a yellow Ford Thunderbird convertible. The girls squealed with joy. Mattie's father had made sure that she would always remember her sixteenth birthday.

Since it was Saturday, there was no school, and with a new car, what more could two young girls wish for than the open road and a long stretch of it to test out the new car's speed and their courage? Turning down the straight path of Route 129, Mattie began to push a little more on the gas pedal. The two girls looked at each other with a "let's do it" expression, and soon they were racing down the road at 100 miles per hour. WOW! It was scary and exciting at the same time, but the fear won out as Mattie dropped back to 55 miles per hour. Both girls were secretly relieved, but definitely more brave and worldly. Should they (or shouldn't they) tell? They decided not to. Their parents were strict and wouldn't often let them go off by themselves even if they obeyed all the rules.

Three months later Nize and Mattie were finally allowed to go for a Sunday afternoon drive with two nice young men. The four of them went for ice cream and a leisurely drive. When they finally turned around to get home, Nize noticed it was already 4:45 p.m., and she panicked because she only had 15 minutes to get home. Nize's mother sternly made it very clear that she was to be home no later than 5:00 p.m. Mattie quickly picked up Nize's expression and asked her, "What's wrong?" Nize pointed to the clock and Mattie took over from there.

She let their dates in on the problem, and the speedometer increased to 60…70.. 80…90…then to 100 mph. The exhilaration of this speed didn't last long, for Nize could see the steering wheel begin to tremble and shake. Seconds later, all four tires squealed, and the next moment seemed to last forever. She felt as though she was in a cement mixer in slow motion, turning over and over. Nize could taste the earth and blood in her mouth, but she couldn't speak. "Dear, God, please protect us," she prayed silently, over and over.

After what seemed an eternity, the car rolled to a stop only inches from a telephone pole at the edge of a cornfield. The car door was jammed shut, but Nize felt someone pulling her through the window, which was now devoid of glass. Two gentlemen from the neighborhood had been driving behind the speeding car and had watched in horror as it came around the sharp curve at high speed. The men picked up Nize and the others, put them into their own car, and rushed the teenagers to the hospital. Nize was in and out of consciousness until she woke up and saw a nurse staring down at her. The nurse left the room to get more gauze, and when she returned, she found Nize lying on the stretcher with her hands folded in prayer.

The nurse smiled to herself and asked, "Nize, are you praying? Don't worry. You are going to be fine, after a few sutures in your forehead." "My friends, where are they?" Nize asked quietly. "In the room next door," the nurse replied. "They have a few bruises and some minor cuts. Your date has a broken arm. I heard the gentlemen who brought you in tell the doctor that the car turned over two times, stood up straight on two wheels and then slammed down and caught on fire. Yep, Nize, you are a lucky group of teenagers." After sharing their experience with the relatives and friends gathered to greet them when they returned home from the hospital that Sunday night, Nize and Mattie both tried to avoid any further conversation on the subject. Late that night, as Nize lay staring at the stars from her bedroom window, she did not forget to thank God that she had survived the crash. The following morning Nize tried to step out of bed but every bone in her body was sore. She tried several times but soon realized that this was going to take another day or two. The day after, she could slowly put one foot in front of the other and painfully take a few steps. It was a week before she could move freely without feeling miserable.

Yes, Nize realized, she had had a close call, and it was many years before she felt comfortable driving around sharp curves again.

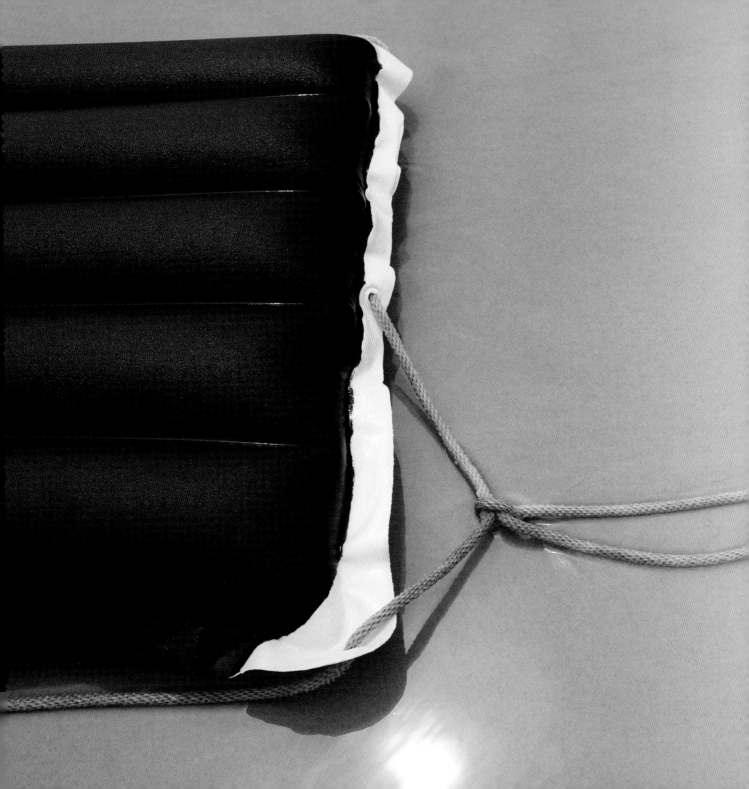

Chapter Seven

The Beach Trip

The class Nize and Mattie were in had planned a trip to the beach. Although Nize lived only a few minutes from the ocean, her parents wouldn't allow her to go alone, but because this trip was for school, they eventually gave permission.

Nize wore her new yellow shorts with a matching yellow shirt that showed her midriff. You couldn't see the two-piece bathing suits she and Mattie had secretly worn underneath their shorts. It was a secret because they were not allowed to go into the water on the beach trip. With twenty-five students going on the trip, it would be too much responsibility for the teachers supervising the students to allow them to go swimming. After a short trip from their school, the students quickly exited the bus and were very excited about being at the beach. The principal, Mr. Smith interrupted their thoughts as he explained that they were only to walk on the beach, dance, eat, and socialize. Each student was to report back to the bus in three hours. The beach pavilion was alive with sounds of beach music from groups likes the Platters and the Drifters. Lots of couples were doing a dance popular to the area called "shagging" in rhythm to the beach music, as the aroma of cotton candy filled the air.

After spending some time chatting with their friends, Nize and Mattie, who had come prepared to get some sun, strolled down the beach, hand in hand. Soon they approached some large sand dunes with lots of sea oats. The girls looked at each other and disappeared behind the tall plants. They reappeared on the other side clad in brightly-colored bathing suits. Nize and Mattie walked toward the water, but decided to sit on the beach strand and sunbathe. After about twenty minutes of sit-

ting
on the warm sand in the
bright sunshine, perspiration was rolling
down their cheeks. Nize and Mattie longingly looked at the cool
ocean, then at each other, and without saying a word, ran into the water, splashing and laughing.

Nize and Mattie were having so much fun and the cool water felt so good that Nize decided to go out a little further so her shoulders would be covered. Suddenly, Nize heard a familiar voice calling her name so she turned toward the shore. "Oh no," Nize moaned. "How in the world did Mr. Smith see me?"

The principal was frantically yelling and pointing at her. It was too late; the giant wave came across her back and knocked her underwater. She tried to get up, only to feel a wall of water above her head. She tried again, but could not break through the surge of water over her. It seemed pretty calm on the bottom. "Could I swim or perhaps crawl to shore? Could I survive without air for that long?" Nize quickly thought to herself. She was so tired and not sure if she was going to make it. "Dear God, help me. Is this the end?" she asked, despairingly. "It feels so strangely peaceful," she thought. As Nize struggled, she felt something pulling her through the huge waves and she came up above the water. Suddenly what should have been sweet relief became the reality of looking into the big, angry eyes of Mr. Smith. He grabbed her by the ear and dragged her to shore. Nize felt

as if she had swallowed the whole ocean during the underwater struggle. As she coughed, the water continued to gush out of her mouth, and she was very weak.

Mr. Smith sat Nize down on the sand and she continued to cough. By now a few classmates had gathered around her. Some were snickering and a few whispered, "Is she okay?" Mattie quickly retrieved her shorts from behind the sea oats. Mr. Smith escorted Nize to the nearest restroom, shoved her in, and slammed the door shut. When Nize finished dressing, she sheepishly opened the door, and without a word, Mr. Smith led her to the chair between Miss Patten and himself. Nize hoped no one would see her—not as long as she lived. Occasionally she did get the courage to look around Mr. Smith's chair to see how Mattie was doing. As they were both being reprimanded and reminded of the dangers and con-sequences of what they had done and how lucky they were, Nize felt Mama's prayers had protected her. Mama had spent many nights praying for her and Roger's safety.

When she got home, she ran into Mama's arms where she felt safe, and Nize hoped Mama would never find out how foolish she had been that day. One thing was for sure, she wouldn't hear it from Nize or Mattie.

Chapter Eight

The Prom

Nize's date for her senior prom was a state college man Roger had introduced to her. Her brother was the only reason her mother had said he could take her to the prom. Nize couldn't wait to wear her gorgeous dress. It was a white strapless affair with net and tulle that went to her ankles and showed off her new white pumps. The shoes had the highest heels Nize had ever been allowed to wear. What type of hairstyle Nize would wear to her senior prom was the last decision to be made that day.

Mattie and Sue had asked Nize to go with them to get new hairstyles for the prom. She had always managed to style her own hair in a medium pageboy style, which was relatively easy to do. But her friends said, "Oh, come along. We won't be long," so Nize decided to keep them company. Little did she know that that minor decision would have an effect on her whole life.

The hairstylist was a middle-aged woman who smoked a lot. Between smoke breaks, she boasted to everyone within earshot about what a great stylist she was. She was also proud of her many years of experience. Her skills seemed adequate and Mattie and Sue were soon finished. Nize genuinely thought they looked beautiful and told them so.

Touching the upswept curls on her head, Mattie looked at Nize and asked, "Why don't you have your hair styled since this is such a special occasion? We only go to the Prom once, and besides, it will be so much quicker this way."

"Oh yes," the older hairstylist said. "I could do wonders with your nice thick hair. I know just what to do." Nize stared at her friends. "Well, maybe," she said reluctantly. With Nize's agreement, the stylist swiftly wrapped the cutting cape around her shoulders and began to snip, snip, snip. She scooped up a handful of styling gel, followed by long metal clips, and soon had Nize under the dryer. An hour later she was sitting in the styling chair staring at her reflection in the mirror. Her first impression was that of a "Roaring '20's Flapper."

Then the stylist turned her for a side view. Pinocchio. The style made her nose look like Pinocchio's nose. Mattie and Sue began to snicker. Nize, having been taught to always have good manners, paid the lady at the counter, thanked her, and then fled outside. Now Mattie and Sue's snickers led to belly laughing. However, they stopped long enough to tell Nize not to worry, that the hairstyle looked okay. They couldn't force themselves to say "pretty."

Finally, in her own room, Nize looked in the mirror and began to weep. According to the clock, she had less than an hour to be dressed and be ready for her date. "Please, dear God. What can I do? Help me. I can't even cancel because he's already on his way to pick me up," she said.

Nize, in her temporary hysteria, reached up and ran her finger through the stiff waves in her hair. Suddenly they started to break apart and her hair became softer and fuller. She grabbed some rollers and quickly wrapped her hair around them. Next, she turned on the shower to get some steam in her hair and then used a little heat from her mother's iron. After letting her hair cool for a few minutes, Nize held her breath as she ran a large comb through it. Immediately, the thick hair framed her face. Just the way Elizabeth Taylor, her favorite actress, wore hers, Nize thought. Nize jumped into her white gown, pushed her feet into her new pumps, and off she went.

Meanwhile, Mattie and Sue had been informing all their classmates of Nize's demise. She would be the joke of the prom. Instead, Nize walked into the school gymnasium on the arm of her date, Ward, the "college man," with her head held high and a big, sly grin on her face. Her classmates stared in wonder and disappointment as she and Ward smoothly danced across the floor to "Smoke Gets in Your Eyes." They danced the night away to all the great tunes by the Platters, the Four Tops, Bill Haley and the Comets, and all the other popular musicians they loved. It was a magical evening for Nize. Everyone was in a romantic mood as the music played late into the night. What could have been a very difficult evening for Nize actually turned into a magical night.

Nize's thoughts went back to everything that had happened that day. "Wouldn't it be nice," she thought, "if I could become a great hair designer - someone who would never disappoint anyone the way I was disappointed today? I bet I could make many people happy. I think I would really like that." She made a note to herself to see what it would take to pursue this career.

Chapter Nine

May

Nize was finally a month away from her high school graduation. She had no way of knowing exactly what that month would have in store for her. About the only thing she could be sure of was that she would not be the valedictorian of her class. Nize's four years of high school had been filled with many things; however, studying had not been her first priority, and she had to work hard at times to keep up her grades. Being the youngest student in her class (and less mature) sometimes made it necessary to cram for exams in order to pass a course. That was all that mattered in her opinion. Laughing with good friends, learning about life, daydreaming, and searching for adventure could be very consuming to a young girl like Nize. She could only hope that the priority she made of her social life would lead her somewhere.

May Day festivities were a big event at Seashore High School. To rule over the event as the May Queen would be a dream come true. That lucky person was elected by the whole student body of Seashore High.

Nize was late getting out of bed and it seemed to take an eternity to get ready for school. Having a bad hair day did not help, but she grabbed her sack of books and headed for the old red Dodge truck. Papa would take her to school since she was running late.

Once there, she tiptoed down the long hall and finally reached her home room. She gently opened the door and walked to her empty seat, wishing no one could see her. The dead silence in the room was not helping the situation. She felt all eyes looking at her. She wished she had just stayed in bed. Just then, Miss Flowers rose from her seat, stood, and looked straight toward Nize.

"Nize, the student body has a surprise for you. They have voted you as our May Queen this year," she said. Still recovering from the hectic morning, it took a few seconds for Nize to catch her breath. She turned, looked around the room, and felt her legs go weak. Tears came to her eyes, as she looked at all the students sitting at their desks in silence. She said, "Thank you," and thought to herself, "I will do my best to look good and be the best May Queen ever." Her teacher and all the students applauded as she sat down.

Nize could hardly wait to get home that afternoon to tell her mother the wonderful news. After all, her mother had stayed up many times until the wee hours of the morning sewing a dress Nize had designed. Mama always worked alongside her daughter until they created something different and outstanding. What outfit would catch the most eyes? She hoped her mother would be up for sewing something really special this time. Nize thought she would take the white strapless dress she had worn to the prom and redesign it to be the prettiest dress any May Queen had ever worn!

There was no sleeping that night until Nize had added layers of net and ruffles to the gown in her mind. She made it into a long, elegant dream of a dress that would be fitting for a queen. Mama did the sewing, while Nize did the designing and the dreaming. With her mother's help, the dress became exactly what she had envisioned.

The day of the big event finally arrived. The Maypoles had long streams of colorful crepe paper ribbons that intertwined as the students danced around them. The music from different countries was lively as groups of students depicted folk dancing from around the world. Then everything stopped as the queen and king walked through the crowd and took seats on their thrones. They were overlooking the events taking place on the large school yard. The photographer continuously clicked his camera, and Nize had never felt more beautiful. Or more happy. Nize's parents were so proud when they opened the next edition of the local newspaper and saw their daughter's picture. Maybe she was finally doing something right or maybe she just got lucky. Nize was unaware of it now, but she was going to need a lot more luck in the not too distant future.

Chapter Ten

The Hurricane

At last Nize and her family had settled into their new home near the beach. It had taken quite a few years to build it. Papa had done the carpentry work and the family took care of all the other work. Like Nize, Papa had a creative side. Although he had to spend most of his days in repetitive farm labor, his artistic gifts would often appear in surprising ways. His carpentry and building talents were unparalleled.

After hours and on weekends he became the neighborhood barber. The men would gather at his house after their day's labor, and share world news while Papa cut their hair with manual hand-held clippers. Never having gone to barber college didn't stop him from helping his neighbors. Love of art prevailed as they socialized, laughed and listened to war news. Many of Nize's days were spent sitting on the floor, looking up, watching Papa cut hair as the old manual clippers went click, click, click.

Papa's family was originally from Boston, Massachusetts, where his ancestors were much less economically challenged than he was. Their successes were nationally recognized as Roger Batson was a national financial advisor, who founded Batson College in Massachusetts, Webber College in Batson Park, Florida, and even had a wing of a local hospital named for the family. Sea captains were also prevalent in the family. Capt. John delivered correspondence between President John Adams and his wife Abigail. Papa's great-great-grandfather, also a sea captain, traveled all the way down the east coast to Brunswick County, North Carolina. There, he fell in love and married a southern girl who refused to set foot on his ship bound north to Boston. He would not leave his new love. This challenged him to learn new skills such as farming, building, wildlife, timber management, and other ways to support the large family they raised. But the sea was still in Papa's genes, and finally moving his family closer to the ocean had been one of his dreams. Nize enjoyed camping with her family and eating their evening meals outside together. The fried chicken, butter beans, sweet potatoes, and banana pudding Mama prepared were as tasty and refreshing as always. The family relaxed after completing long hours working on the house each day.

Living near the beach was different than living inland. The cool breeze at night was so tranquilizing that Nize slept like a baby and always woke up refreshed and ready for some new adventure. The best part was sitting with Mattie, who often came to visit, at sunset and watching the huge orange sun drift slowly down until it appeared to sink into the ocean and out of sight. Everything seemed just perfect. But life as Nize knew it was about to take an unexpected turn. Papa raised the volume of the radio as the weatherman reported that a severe hurricane named "Hazel" was about to make landfall along the Carolina coast. Hazel was not far away and would hit the area sometime during that October 1953 night. Papa immediately began nailing boards over all the windows while Mama filled containers with water and carried anything outdoors that was of any value into the house.

Nize sat beside Papa as he quickly drove the old red truck to town. Like Papa, many people were frantically buying batteries, extra groceries, first aid kits, and whatever supplies seemed necessary to ensure survival after Hurricane Hazel. Many people bought candles and kerosene lamps, and all the local folks seemed worried and preoccupied by the coming storm.

As Papa's old truck pulled back into their driveway, Nize noticed that some of the neighbors had come over while she and her father were in town. Since Papa had constructed a very sturdy house, the neighbors thought it would be safer there. Nize's family assured them they were always welcome at their home but especially now that the hurricane was approaching.

Soon the wind began to howl outside of the house as Nize, her family, and some neighbors sat on the floor. The limited view from the window became darker and darker as the people inside Nize's house could only see limbs flying by in the heavy rains brought on by the hurricane. Since the noise was so loud and distracting, no one tried to make any conversation. Nize bowed her head and silently repeated the Lord's Prayer until she began to doze off sometime before daybreak. Gradually, the noise died down, and Papa cracked open the front door ever so slightly. The yard was filled with furniture, pots and pans, as well as uprooted trees and other debris. Everyone carefully made their way outside and to the banks of the Intracoastal Waterway. There they saw lots of furniture, mattresses, dishes, clothes, pictures, and almost anything one could imagine floating in the water.

An old gentleman reached down and pulled something from the debris-filled water. It was a portrait of his sister, who like so many others, was never found. The man quickly realized the tragedy of her death as tears streamed down his weathered face.Months later things had started to get back to normal. Papa had repaired the damage to the roof, and the debris had been cleared away from the yard. Everyone in Nize's neighborhood had pitched in to help each other through the storm. Hurricane Hazel would be remembered for many years. Eventually, Nize and Mattie were able to sit and enjoy the beautiful sunsets. As she looked around at her family and friend who were all safe and sound, she gazed up to the sky and said softly, "Thanks."

Chapter Eleven

Graduation

Elvis was king, the Civil Rights movement was just beginning, space travel was becoming a reality, and Nize was graduating from high school. She felt the whole world changing, and she could barely control her excitement and amazement. Nize wore a new white dress with pink ribbons running through the lace trim, though no one could see it beneath her long red graduation gown. The mortar board was topped with a long tassel that bobbed up and down as she turned to study each of her classmates. This graduating class at Seashore High School looked small when compared to the large graduating class at State College where Nize had recently attended Ward's graduation. He proposed that same day, but she hadn't answered him. She needed time to think. Though she was excited, graduation from high school seemed like small potatoes compared to seeing Ward graduate from college and hearing him propose.

It was no wonder Nize found the boys in her class to be so immature and boring, she thought, looking around her at the pranks and sniggering going on around her. There was no comparison between high school boys and college men. The younger boys just weren't worldly enough for her. Nize wanted to see the big, exciting life ahead of her, and the sooner she experienced it, the better. The diploma she had received would surely be the ticket that would take her away from this small town life. She held the diploma close to her heart as she and her classmates walked toward their future, while the school band played, "Pomp and Circumstance." Nize felt sure she was walking away from a safe and secure place into an uncertain future, but she was prepared and equipped to meet any challenge—or so she thought.

Chapter Twelve

The Dream

After the excitement of her high school graduation, Nize slept soundly in her comfortable featherbed, but her dreams were not so restful. In them, she stood by Ward as the minister pronounced them husband and wife. Nize giggled through the entire wedding ceremony, while Ward, on the other hand, was sober and stern.

The dream seemed to fast forward through the years of their marriage, and Ward continued to be harsh and serious. He considered himself "boss" and controlled Nize in their union. Ward's frequent temper tantrums came at unexpected times and seemed to be brought on by the most trivial things. Some of his tirades resulted in overturned furniture and even flying objects. It was all vivid and frightening.

Nize dreamed she was rocking twins, a boy and a girl, when Ward burst through the door carrying a long, ugly knife. He came toward Nize and her babies. She ran through the back door carrying the twins in her arms, but Ward caught up and was standing over them. Nize screamed for help at the top of her lungs.

Suddenly, someone was shaking her. What a relief it was to open her eyes and see Mama desperately trying to wake her up from the terrible nightmare she was having. As she lay there and thought about what a future with Ward might be like, Nize realized it wasn't what she wanted. She had been impressed by his worldliness and knowledge of things. After all, he was a "college man" and she was only a high school senior. But now Nize knew immediately what she had to do.

At daybreak, pen in hand, Nize wrote Ward a "Dear John, letter, then ran to the mailbox so she could end the relationship as soon as possible. Nize promised herself she would wait until the time was right to get married and settle down. Her nightmare had shocked her into realizing Ward was not the one for her. Nize hoped that he could eventually forgive her, but for now, she just wanted some time to have fun with Mattie and her other friends. After all, she had worked hard to finish high school and she needed a break.

Chapter Thirteen

Leaving Home

The days after high school graduation flew by and before Nize knew it, it was time to pack for the state college in Raleigh her mother had made her apply for earlier in the spring. Nize had dragged her feet since graduation, as she really couldn't see herself leaving all the things she enjoyed so much, like the comfort of laughing with Papa and seeing Mattie. She liked to fantasize about leaving home and going to college, but now the actual situation was not making her as happy as she thought it would. Nize decided she would try one last time to reason with Mama to let her stay home for one year before going off to college. "After all, I was the youngest one in my class to graduate," she pleaded, "and I have plenty of time to go to college."

The stern look on Mama's face did not change as she said, "No, Nize, this is the way we planned it, and this is the way it is going to be. Look at me, Nize, old before my time from doing hard labor on the farm. Is that what you want? You have a great opportunity, and you will go! Help me pack your things."

Nize felt unloved and alone. "Why does Mama want me out of the house? Was I that bad?" Nize asked herself.

Mama closed the lid on the large, cardboard suitcase, saying, "Come help me cook dinner. That will help get your mind on something else."

Nize - The Making of a Champion   **47**

As Nize lay in her bed that night, she could hear Papa walking the floor. She knew he had a lot of fears about his only daughter going to the big city alone, but Mama usually had the final say in matters about Nize and her future. She thought of going to him and begging him to let her stay, but she knew Mama would have her way in the end.

Papa's sister Aunt Madge knew the big city of Raleigh well, so she picked Nize up the next morning to take her to college. The tears flowed freely as Nize looked back longingly at the house and life she loved so dearly. Aunt Madge sized up the situation and tuned the radio to a station that was playing "Jailhouse Rock."

"You know I was scared too," Aunt Madge said over Elvis's rock and roll, "when I started college." She looked over at her niece, then back at the road. "And you know, girls didn't go off to college then. It took a lot of guts, but I did it, and I never looked back."

Aunt Madge put her hand over Nize's smaller one. "And I've never been sorry. You're going to be just fine, honey."

Slowly, Nize was starting to feel better about leaving home.

After a few hours, they arrived at college. Aunt Madge helped Nize settle in and even appointed her a chaperone. She slipped some money into her hand and told Nize to report any problems to the chaperone who was an old college friend of Aunt Madge's. That being done, Nize was on her own for the first time in her life on the first day of college.

Nize's roommate was a girl named Nancy. Nancy had a very modern haircut and all "store-bought" clothes, while poor Nize stood in the dorm room wearing a simple dress her Mama had lovingly made for her. Nize felt even worse when she looked at all the beautiful leather luggage Nancy was now unpacking.

Nize looked at her own large cardboard suitcase filled with homemade dresses and wished the floor would open up and swallow her. Nancy must have sensed Nize's dilemma and started a conversation to reassure her new roommate. "Nize," she said, "I think you'll like it here. I've only been here for a year, and I really love it. Hurry up and unpack and I'll take you to meet some of my friends."

Nize couldn't believe the size of the campus and how many buildings there were. It was certainly not like the farm back home on the coast. Nize and Nancy went to the cafeteria for lunch and Nancy introduced her to some friends. They seemed nice enough, and they didn't laugh at Nize even though they might have wanted to. Nize's first day at college hadn't gone as badly as it could have, she thought, as she fell asleep that night from fatigue.

Daybreak found Nize working on her own transformation. Luckily, she had brought Mama's sewing scissors with her, and she clipped off her hair until it became a masterpiece. With the scissors still in hand, she proceeded to alter the dress she would wear to her first day of classes. She looked at her reflection in the mirror and thought, "Well, this might help."

As it turned out, her beautifying efforts definitely helped, as she enjoyed the admiring glances from passing students while walking to her class. This gave her the confidence she needed to get through her first day. From then on, Nize had to allow time to style her hair and alter her clothes to be more original, noticeable, and to keep up with the latest styles. Nize quickly managed to be the envy of her classmates and often helped them style their hair and clothes. Finally, she felt accepted by the other students and she realized it was worth all the extra effort.

Nize began to adjust to college life, but still, occasionally, she would remember Papa, the sea breeze, and the old red truck. In time, the glamour of college life won out, and to her surprise, Nize started to function as a normal college student.

Chapter Fourteen

College

Soon, the monotony of tests, studying, and dorm food wore on Nize. She was bored. "How can I survive my freshman year here at State without going crazy?" she thought.

One day during the first semester, Nize sat in the student union studying the students as they strolled by her. Nize imagined them with different hairstyles, different makeup, and even sometimes plastic surgery. Her real skills were very much in demand back at the dorm where she lived with other girls.

Unlike friends who belonged to a sorority, Nize's budget would never allow her that luxury. However she had dreams of some day having beautiful clothes like those she saw the coeds on campus wearing. She still wore some of her old clothes from high school. Mama sent handmade clothing when she could, but her health was not so good these days. Nize knew her parents made sacrifices just to pay her tuition, and for that she would always be grateful.

She always had her dreams, though. Nize could always imagine herself to be whatever she wanted to be, and no one could take that away from her. She was always at her best in her world of fantasy, and the daydreams entered her mind frequently these days. In her real life, she began to think of pursuing a part-time job in order to buy clothes and make up for her new college co-ed lifestyle.

One day Nize was reading the classified ads in the campus newspaper when her eyes fell on one particular ad. "Receptionist wanted for large beauty salon downtown." Immediately, Nize went to the location listed and met the salon owner, Mrs. Carrington, a pretty and pleasant lady. After just one conversation, she said Nize could work every Saturday.

Nize was happy to get the job. The salon was in a large, old, southern house on the busy college street. The kind lady who hired Nize said her duties would be mostly to assist her since the State Board would not allow Nize to do anything else without a license. Getting a license would involve going to school for many hours and passing the cosmetology state board exam. But even without that training, Nize knew that the experience would be good, and she would be earning a small wage, which was what she really needed.

Mrs. Carrington smiled a lot and seemed happy most of the time. The customers in the salon laughed and had a good time with her. She didn't seem to have to concentrate very hard as she worked, and Nize assumed that talent came from many years of experience.

One afternoon after all the customers had left, Nize was cleaning the brushes while Mrs. Carrington went into the lady's room. It had a large door with a glass window above it common to a lot of old, southern houses. Nize had finished with the brushes, swept the hair from the floor, and cleaned the rollers, but Mrs. Carrington had not emerged from the lady's room. Nize started to worry about her boss.

"Should I call out to her?" Nize thought, realizing something must be wrong with Mrs. Carrington. Nize called out to her and when there was no answer, she called her name in a louder voice. Nize was frightened and decided she had to do something. Pulling a large chair to the door, she stood on it on her tiptoes and looked through the glass window above the door. There on the floor lay Mrs. Carrington, looking like she was dead.

Nize jumped back from the sight below her, and she knew what she had to do. Her boss could be having a heart attack, Nize thought, as she frantically called for an ambulance. After twenty agonizing minutes, the men came in, broke down the bathroom door, and put Mrs. Carrington's seemingly lifeless body onto a stretcher for the trip to the emergency room. Nize insisted that she come along and stayed by her boss's side from the salon until she was taken into one of the treatment rooms at the hospital. After a long wait, the doctor entered with Mrs. Carrington staggering behind him.

The doctor, shaking his head in anger, said to Nize, "Get this woman out of here. She's intoxicated!"

Nize was completely shocked, but she tried not to show it in front of her boss who wouldn't look her in the eye. Nize called a cab and Mrs. Carrington followed behind her to the waiting car.

On the ride back to the salon, Mrs. Carrington said, "Nize, have you ever seen a drunk?" Nize shook her head. "Well, I'll forgive you this time, but don't ever do this to me again. I should make you pay the emergency room bill," Mrs. Carrington said angrily.

After that, Nize didn't waste any time. The next day she went downtown to a nice salon in a department store and applied for a job. The lady, short of help that day, asked Nize, "Did you bring a uniform?"

Nize replied, "No, but I'll get one." After running off to another department of the store, Nize donned her new clothes and returned to the salon. Nize began working in a more sober atmosphere, but she would never forget her experience with Mrs. Carrington. Sometimes she sill felt bad for her because she was really a very pleasant lady.

In the salon, something about the constant ring of the cash register and the happy smiles on the faces of the clients when they looked at their reflection in the mirror made Nize's courses at the college seem more boring than they already were. It was enough to lead her to the local cosmetology college to enroll as a part time student. Her plan was to eventually earn a degree in cosmetology as well as keep up her studies at State. She worked at night and on Saturdays. It meant no social life, but Nize was more interested in achieving her financial independence right now than going out on dates.

Many nights, Nize studied almost until dawn, and youth was on her side. At least that's what she thought until the morning she couldn't pull herself out of bed. Nancy insisted she go to the college infirmary. Though she was reluctant, Nize agreed to go and dragged herself there that afternoon.

Chapter Fifteen

The Intern

Nize noticed the smell of hospital and sickness in the college infirmary, and she was relieved when her name was finally called. In the examining room she was told to take her clothes off, put on a gown, and sit on the white linen-covered table. An old doctor came in and listened to Nize's chest.

Unexpectedly, a young man wearing a white lab coat came into the exam room. His tousled hair had golden sun streaks that enhanced the dark suntan on his face, where the bluest eyes Nize had ever seen stared at her. Nize felt as if those beautiful eyes could see right through her. She began to clutch at the front of the hospital gown she was wearing, trying to hide as much as possible while a stethoscope was pressed against her chest.

The doctor looked at the young intern and said, "Classic case of extreme fatigue. We see this often here because students don't get enough rest, don't eat right, or just don't take care of their health." The young man looked at Nize and told her to go back to her dorm and get some rest, and the doctors left her alone to dress.

All the next week, for some strange reason, Nize found herself going over and over all the emotions she had felt in the infirmary the day she met that handsome intern. It was as though she didn't want to let go of the way those blue eyes had met hers when he kindly told her to get some rest.

Summer break was fast approaching, and Nize didn't run into the young doctor again that semester. She was looking forward to her time back at the beach, away from school. The ocean and her home had always washed away her fatigue and restored her. She closed her eyes and imagined the warm sunshine on her face and the soft breeze blowing through her hair. Suddenly Nize could breathe easier, even in the stuffy classroom.

Chapter Sixteen

Myrtle Beach

Papa's older sister Madge had done pretty well for herself in life. She and her husband owned a beach front hotel in Myrtle Beach, South Carolina, and when her husband passed away, she became the sole owner of the hotel. After several years, Aunt Madge recovered from his unexpected death and became an avid golfer and local country club socialite.

Nize was very much like her aunt. She had Madge's personality as well as some of her physical features. Everyone in the family noticed how much the two were alike which is probably why Nize was Madge's favorite niece. It was not unusual for Nize to get an invitation to spend Spring Break at her aunt's hotel, where she could get some rest.

The bus ride from college to the beach had been long and tiresome, so the sights and smells of the large dining room at the county club were a welcome sight for Nize. Aunt Madge had ordered sherry earlier for Nize's special arrival, and she and Nize drank a toast to the weekend.

Casting a critical gaze on Nize's faded jeans, Aunt Madge mentioned the wonderful dress store her friend owned in town. She also told Nize that since the big dance was Saturday night, they should go shopping for new dresses early the next morning. Of course, Aunt Madge would be buying the dress.

As they walked toward the exit, Nize had a big smile on her face when she happened to spot two golfers walking into the dining room and toward a table by the windows. Nize felt faint as she looked into the face of that same young man with the blue eyes who she had seen just a few weeks earlier in the college infirmary. He was holding two golf gloves in one hand as Nize and Madge passed them, and he turned around quickly as though he had forgotten something. The young doctor smiled into her eyes and nodded, holding out a golf glove toward Nize. "Would you like to play a round of golf?" he asked simply.

Nize's face turned beet red and she was speechless. Aunt Madge came to her rescue by telling him that they had a previous appointment, knowing full well that Nize knew absolutely nothing about the game of golf. Nize looked back and smiled at him as she walked away, murmuring, "Sorry." She tightly clutched the glove she had completely forgotten she was holding.

The next morning Aunt Madge and Nize chose a beautiful white dress for the dance from her friend's shop. They had just returned to the hotel when they were surprised in the lobby by the young intern. He unabashedly walked up to them, and after a cheerful "Good morning," looked straight into Nize's eyes and said, "My name is Andy and I was wondering if you could show me around Myrtle Beach today?"

Nize looked pleadingly at Aunt Madge, who smiled at both of them and said to Nize, "Show Andy our wonderful beach."

Nize was on cloud nine as she flew up to her room and returned just three minutes later wearing a cover-up over a modest bathing suit. Andy and Nize made small talk as they walked toward the beach. However, the small talk soon accelerated into happy conversation, and it wasn't long before they realized they shared many of the same goals, values, and tastes. The air became warmer, which made the water so inviting that they had to run into the cool waves. They swam until the aroma of hot dogs wafted toward them from the pavilion. Soon they had their fill of delicious hot dogs, french fries, and cold soft drinks. "Now, what is the most fun here in Myrtle Beach?" Andy asked Nize.

She hesitated. "The most exciting thing I've ever done here?" she asked. "My Dad took me on a ride one summer," she said, smiling mischievously. "What kind of ride?" Andy asked. "A helicopter," she replied. Andy laughed with surprise. They drove to a small airport that was nearby and were escorted into a large rental helicopter. Once Nize and Andy were airborne, the views of Myrtle Beach were magnificent. It was such a thrill, and when the helicopter encountered some turbulence, Andy put his arm around Nize. They were sitting so close that when he turned toward her everything became still, and he kissed her lips lightly. It was so shocking that they both tried to pull away, but instead another jolt of turbulence pressed them closer, and their lips met again for a long and blissful kiss. Afterward, they put their arms around each other and held tight until they felt the helicopter landing back at the airport. When their feet touched the ground, Nize and Andy were still dizzy, and they walked on air back to the hotel. Strange emotions had overwhelmed them both, and they knew they should call it a day. "Will I see you at the dance?" asked Andy.

"Yes, you will," Nize assuredly replied as Andy very slowly walked her back to her room. The events of the past few hours had left them speechless. Feelings like this were not ones they particularly cared to discuss. How could they? Neither of them quite understood it yet, and they certainly didn't want to admit it, even to themselves.

Chapter Seventeen

The Dance

The strapless white summer dress complemented Nize's suntan from a day at the beach as she stood waiting for Andy to arrive at the dance. Across the room, Aunt Madge waltzed on the beautiful dance floor. As Nize studied the artwork on the ballroom wall, she felt a tap on her shoulder. Andy greeted her with a polite, "Good evening, Nize." He led her to the dance floor as the band played "Only You," by the Platters, the song that had played in her imagination through every romantic dream she'd ever had.

They stopped dancing to have champagne, and after a few more songs, they went outside for a breath of fresh air. Both of their heads were spinning from the effects of the bubbly drinks. They could hear the soft music from the country club as they walked along the beach in the moonlight. As Andy leaned over and kissed her beneath the stars, it seemed to Nize as though they were the only two people on the planet. Nothing mattered except this night, this sand beneath their feet, and the feelings they had for each other. The world stopped for a while as Nize and Andy were united in love.

Everything was wonderful until the next morning when Nize woke up in her hotel room—alone and with an excruciating headache. She soon realized that her magical night with Andy had resulted in her losing what Mama had preached to her about protecting. How could she feel so much pure love for Andy and feel so terrible about what had happened at the same time? Nize's mother had instilled in her the need to protect something so precious and save it for the man she decided to marry. Nize heard a knock at her room door. "Could it be Andy?" she thought. "Surely he will make everything alright," Nize was thinking as she opened the door.

A note had just been slipped under her door.

Hospital had an emergency.
Had to drive back early this morning.
I'm so sorry.
I'll call.
Love, Andy

Nize felt sad and very alone. She reached for the golf glove Andy had given her yesterday at the country club. She put it on her hand for comfort as the tears started slowly rolling down her cheeks. Except for a short visit with Mama and Papa, Nize spent the rest of her spring break sitting alone on the beach. She was afraid to spend a lot of time with her parents because she was afraid they would figure out her secret and she just couldn't disappoint them. "They can't ever know," she promised herself. "They won't."

She only hoped that she was right.

Chapter Eighteen

Andy

Andy was called back to State due to a big fire in one of the dorms. Both the infirmary and the hospital needed all available doctors and interns to help take care of the overflow of students wounded by the fire. Andy worked almost two days without any sleep. The tragic situation was finally under control and now Andy went outside for some fresh air. As he walked around, he saw the flickering lights of a diner. Although it was midnight, Andy had barely eaten in two days, and the grumbling in his stomach was all he could think about.

As Andy walked down the street toward the diner, his thoughts went back to Myrtle Beach. He sorely missed Nize. He had never before felt this way about any girl. "Have I fallen in love with her?" Andy asked himself. He wondered if Nize would understand that the duties of his job forced him to leave so abruptly. He thought surely by now Nize had read his note and heard about the fire on campus. Andy didn't want Nize to think anything negative about him, especially since she had been on his mind since the first day he met her in the infirmary. Andy wondered if Nize felt the same. He thought she did after the night on the beach although the champagne had greatly accelerated what happened. He sincerely hoped she felt the same special feelings for him that he felt for her. Andy had never before felt this way—scared and happy at the same time. He promised himself he would call Nize first thing tomorrow morning and smiled at the thought of hearing her voice.

Andy sat alone in the crowded diner and was enjoying the smell of bacon frying. He was starting to relax when two men burst into the front door with stockings over their heads. As the robbers ran toward the cash register with guns pointed, the lady behind it froze. "Open it!" one of the robbers yelled. She didn't move. "I said, open it or we will shoot," the man shouted frantically.

Andy thought, "I've got to help her." He knew the robbers would shoot the lady if she didn't give them the money, so Andy rose from his seat and almost immediately felt a burning sensation in his side. He turned, and felt another sharp pain, this time in his back, and then everything went black as he fell to the floor.

 When Andy woke up, he found himself lying in a hospital bed, with a kind-faced doctor standing over him. "How do you feel, Andy?" asked the doctor.
"Where am I?" he asked groggily.

"You're in the best hospital in the country," Dr. Moore answered. "You were flown here last night and we did surgery to remove the bullets. We've done all we can do now."

Andy asked the doctor, "What happened, did they shoot her?"

"No," the doctor told Andy. "The newspaper article said they thought you had a gun and they ran, but not before one of them shot you. The paper said you saved her life. You're a hero, Andy." Exhausted from the short conversation, Andy went back to sleep.

Sometime later, he heard someone calling him so he opened his eyes. It was his father, but he looked very sad as he reached down to hug him. As his dad was holding him, something told Andy to move his legs. He tried but didn't feel them move so he reached down to touch them but couldn't feel them. "Dad," he asked, "what's wrong with my legs?"

His father shook his head sadly. "One of the bullets came too close to your spine," he explained. "Don't worry, Andy, we'll beat this. You've never let anything keep you down before, and now you're facing a big challenge. Together we'll conquer this."

Thus began a tremendous challenge that lasted for several years as Andy bravely endured therapy. His thoughts continued to remain on Nize but he couldn't bring himself to call her. Not as long as he was like this. Not until he had won this battle. He prayed she wouldn't forget him and that some day he could stand on his legs, walk up to her, and start where they had left off. He could not give up until he walked again, no matter how long that might take.

Would Nize wait for him? She was constantly on Andy's mind. He could not bear the possibility that he could be crippled and thus a burden on Nize. No, he would have to get better, and then, somehow, he would find her. He would not allow himself to accept any alternative.

Chapter Nineteen

Isabel

The nine months since Nize's trip to Myrtle Beach had been long, and she had done a lot of soul searching. Nize hadn't heard anything from Andy since the night he left. She was too proud to try and contact him, so she tried to forget about him.

Now she found herself on the delivery room table in the maternity ward in an out-of-town hospital. She had asked God to forgive her for being so foolish and to please ease the terrible pain she was now experiencing.

After what seemed an eternity of agony, a beautiful little girl made her way into the world. "You could call her Isabel, Nize" Aunt Madge suggested. "Our first ancestor was a lady named Isabel. She came from England and settled in Boston. She made quite a name for herself in the field of medicine and was well respected in Boston. Our little Isabel wouldn't do so bad to follow in those footsteps."

Nize smiled and nodded in approval to her aunt, thankful that she had her constant love and support. She promised little Isabel she would have a good and respectful life. Nize promised she would devote her life to Isabel, doing whatever she needed to do to make the best for her daughter. Exhausted, Nize told herself she would start making plans tomorrow, but today she just needed to rest.

Nize had been a strong-willed child, but she had much compassion in her heart and didn't want to disappoint her parents. Aunt Madge had arranged for her to have the baby at an out of town hospital. Now it was over, and Nize was relieved that her parents had not been hurt by her mistake. Nize made excuses as to why she could not visit her parents. Luckily, they thought she was just too busy with school and work. She would tell them when the time was right.

Chapter Twenty

Changes

Nize decided she would give up college at State and make a career in cosmetology, which would be the quickest way to make the most money. Cosmetology would be harder work and not as prestigious as a career in medicine, but Nize vowed she would be the best. She felt her decision to pursue this career would be a rewarding one once she learned the skills of the cosmetology field.

As Nize embarked on her new journey, Aunt Madge often took care of Isabel, and Nize spent as much time with her as she possibly could. Taking Isabel to the nursery was always painful, not just for Nize but also for Isabel. It saddened Nize to have to leave her precious daughter there, but she knew she had to work in order to take care of Isabel.

Nize's full-time job at the salon required her to work long hours standing on her feet. Sometimes her days lasted twelve hours, but Nize learned skills that would never fail her in her chosen career. After she had worked for some time, the local Cosmetology College encouraged her to teach. She was serious about academics and studied through many long nights so she could pass her State Board exams, which were all that stood in the way of getting her teacher's license. When she triumphantly passed, Nize was excited to begin the next phase of her career.

Nize's first job as a teacher was in a very pleasant college of cosmetology. The school's owner, Mr. Truman, was compassionate and kind and always made time for both his students and his teachers. Everyone who was involved with the college enjoyed the very harmonious and relaxed atmosphere.

Teaching was both challenging and rewarding to Nize. The students found Nize's classes fun and interesting, especially cosmetic chemistry. She taught her students the pH of hair and products. The students were always delighted when Nize shocked them with dramatic chemical reactions that simulated the way cosmetology really works. One of their favorite examples involved adding high pH soap to a jar of water. The jar, after a little shake, became full of huge, round bubbles. Then Nize would add vinegar, to neutralize the soap, which made the bubbles shrink and then disappear.

Nize, however, wanted to push her students further to challenge them, and after she and Mr. Truman had a long conversation one evening, a decision was made to enter three students in the upcoming state cosmetology competition.

Nize and her students were very excited and worked hard to create three beautiful models for the competition. Mr. Truman was supportive of everyone's hard work without putting any real pressure on them to bring home first place, though he knew the college would benefit from the publicity. The cosmetology teams were much like sports competitors. Winning teams—in football, basketball or cosmetology—made the school look good and resulted in increased enrollment for the programs.

Nize had natural talent and with her knowledge of new trends and techniques soon her students were also winning awards. After extensive training, Nize's students would sometimes win all levels of the contest—first, second, and third place. Nize was proud of all of them, and she was sure it was just the beginning of a long line of triumphs.

Chapter Twenty-one

Missing Child

Nize still took regular customers while she was teaching at the college, and the last one that day, Mrs. Brown, had been a problem. She was forty minutes late, which was out of the ordinary, and on top of that, Nize couldn't get her hair to process correctly. Taking some extra time with her customer would surely make her late picking up Isabel at the nursery. Nize finally decided to turn Mrs. Brown over to one of her co-workers so she could go and pick up her daughter.

Nize rushed from the salon and tried to make up some of the time, but traffic was unusually heavy. When she reached the nursery and found everyone gone, Nize started to panic. After running up the steps, she a heard a noise in the bathroom and found it was only the maid cleaning the sink. Even with some smooth talking, Nize was only able to get the maid to reveal that she really didn't know where the nursery owner had taken Isabel. In a panic, Nize found the phone directory and frantically looked up the owner's number and address. The phone rang for a long time and no one answered.

Nize jumped in her car and drove as fast as she could, praying constantly. She found the nursery owner's house and without even taking time to ring the doorbell, flung open the door. Nize saw the most beautiful sight she had ever seen–Isabel sitting on the floor as if nothing was wrong, quietly playing with a rag doll. Nize quickly swept Isabel up into her arms and held her tightly as tears of relief and joy ran down her face. Nize thanked the nursery owner while she held her daughter close.

"Thank God you're safe," Nize whispered to Isabel, as she put her in the car. She hated to let go of her to drive, but composed herself enough to do so. Nize kept tenderly touching her as she drove home.

That night while trying to go to sleep, Nize made a decision she had been thinking about for a very long time. Nize decided it was time for Isabel to meet her grandparents. Nize hoped her parents would forgive her for things that happened in the past. She knew she had to give her parents the opportunity to see their granddaughter. Although she was afraid of bringing them shame or of how they might react, Nize finally mustered up the courage to tell them she had a child.

When she broke the news to her parents, Mama just stood there in shock, her angry eyes boring into Nize. This secret was very hard for Mama to understand and accept. Papa, on the other hand, just watched his beautiful little granddaughter with a soft smile. Only a few minutes passed before Isabel was sitting on his knee sipping cold Coca Cola from his favorite coffee cup. With each sip, Papa would coach Isabel to show how much she liked cola by saying "Ahh, ahh." Papa laughed each time she drank from the cup and made noises.

Finally, Mama couldn't resist Isabel's charm any more and moved closer to where Isabel was sitting. She stroked her curly hair and eventually brought her onto her lap. Nize let out a long-held breath of relief and knew she had done the right thing.

Mama and Papa took Isabel outside and introduced her to their animals. That night, after Isabel was asleep, both Mama and Papa insisted Nize leave Isabel with them for a little while. Nize happily agreed to her parents' idea. Nize could tell that her parents were happy, but she would always feel like she had disappointed them. She knew she had to make it up to them. She had to make a success of herself. For them, and for Isabel.

Isabel spent some happy time with her grandparents while Nize continued to work long hours. Nize realized how truly lucky she was to have such good parents who believed in her dreams and did all they could to help her achieve them. Aunt Madge had seen her through some rough times and now Nize's parents were there for her. "Yes, I am a blessed woman," she thought and vowed that someday, somehow, she would repay them for all they had done for her.

Chapter Twenty-two

Growth

As Nize kept working as hard as she could at the cosmetology college, her students continued winning competitions all over the state. One of the contests Nize took them to would have a profound effect on her own life.

The large hotel ballroom at the state competition was crowded as Nize's three well-trained students finished their comb-outs. The students left the room so the judges could pick three winners from the large field of models in the competition. When the judges left the room, all the contestants' models were asked to parade for the audience. As her three models appeared on the runway, it seemed to Nize that the applause was louder, and she heard some of the people in the audience say how original and beautiful her students' models hair styles were. Nize heard words from the crowd like "different" and "so pretty," and she could see with her own eyes that her models were accurately described.

The judges finally posted the scores, and Nize quickly went to see the results. Nize gasped in horror as she read the scores and saw that none of her lovely models had received a winning score! Out of the corner of her eye she spotted one of the judges and felt the blood rushing to her face as she pushed her way through the crowd toward the small female judge with blonde hair. Nize was not usually one to speak out in a crowd, but since she had inherited her Papa's quick temper, she got right in the judge's face and said, "I am very angry. Could you explain my students' scores?"

The judge was backing away when Nize felt a very strong hand pressing oh her shoulder. Nize turned and looked into the eyes of a middle-aged gentleman who looked as if he had just come off the cover of Esquire Men's Magazine. The man's suit and tie spoke money and success.

He chuckled to himself as he said, "Calm down, young lady, I can explain all this to you if you will please calm down." Nize stared hard at his face, and he continued talking to her. "Your work is very good, but you were not within the guidelines for this trend competition." Nize had a puzzled look on her face as the man placed his business card in her hand. "Come to my college tomorrow, I can help you better understand," he said before he walked away.

Nize looked at the card and the realized who the well-dressed man was. He was the owner of the cosmetology college a few blocks down the street from her school. She had a lot of trouble sleeping that night but by dawn it was clear to her. At nine o'clock, she was sitting across from Mr. Esquire.

"You have natural talent," he said, "and you are also hungry. I see some of who I used to be in you," he told her. "Let me show you what I can do for you." Nize followed the owner as he showed her new technology she had never seen, new trends with directions from the National Cosmetology Association, videos from the best programs in the country.

Mr. Esquire said, "I will supply you with a Pivot Point education but the rest is up to you." Nize had read about the Pivot Point International School method of teaching cosmetology before, and now she would have a chance to learn the method for herself. As if learning Pivot Point was not enough for Nize, the salary he wrote down on the piece of paper he handed her cinched the deal.

Now Nize had something hard to do. She had to say goodbye to her first college employer, who she really respected and cared for a great deal. But it was the time to move on. If Nize could have seen the future that day she would have been relieved to know she would cross paths with her first employer in later years in a very successful professional venture, but today it was very difficult to say goodbye. Her first boss had been kind and helpful, and Nize had learned a great deal about both people and business from him.

In Mr. Esquire's college, the rules were more rigid, the work much harder, the hours longer, and the competition greater between the teachers. Nize was the newest teacher and vowed to do her best. When Nize was promoted to styles director, one of the school's teachers was angry and left the college. The teacher returned to the school when she realized Nize was not the enemy, but actually an asset to the school

Nize began to train students to win trophies for the college, and soon all the teachers began to respect Nize's hard work and ability, as the school's enrollment rapidly increased. At times things were tough. Accommodating the different personalities of the staff was difficult, but Nize always made a special effort to be nice as well as helpful to everyone. Nize saw lots of judges since she entered her students in many competitions, and one night she saw the lady judge she had once spoken to so angrily. Nize promptly walked up to the lady judge and apologized to her for her past rudeness. Nize told her she now understood the competition rules.

"That's alright, dear," the old woman said before turning away.
"You were right; yours **were** better."

Nize grew professionally in the next few years as her students won many competitions. Nize attributed her success in teaching cosmetology to two things—having learned the Pivot Point system and having joined the National Cosmetology Association.

After attending many competitions with her students, Nize came to the realization she had to win some upper level competitions herself if her career was to advance as far as she needed it to. Nize began to search for the right model on whom she could demonstrate her talent. The woman needed to have good hair, good bone structure, patience, and the time to sit for long hours of practice. Nize searched her students and the patrons on the school's clinic floor, until finally one day she lucked out. Across the room, Nize spotted a woman, and she instantly knew she had found her "perfect model." She was ready to begin the next phase of her career.

Chapter Twenty-three

What Makes a Champion?

In Nize's ongoing quest for truth in the pursuit of winning competitions, she was forever searching for answers and methods to victory. She began to seek and obtain the important credentials that make a champion. She found the soul of a champion was far from ordinary. It's what's inside of you, how much you are willing to do, and how much you are willing to sacrifice that makes a champion. Nize read that there were several mental and emotional characteristics common to champions.

Competitiveness, Nize learned, was being motivated to test your skills against the next person or digging deeper than an opponent. Confidence, specifically, self-confidence, was a belief in one's own ability to perform, and seeing one's self as a winner was a necessary attribute to a champion. Though she had gained great confidence, Nize was, and taught her students to be, extremely humble. Even if she felt sure her students would win, you could never be totally sure, so she kept quiet and prayed. Nize found composure helped her keep herself together under pressure, especially if she made a wrong move. You could still pull things together in the final minutes of a competition without falling apart. You could deal with mistakes and not get rattled so you could focus and pay attention to what was most important. If you were distracted, you could refocus quickly. Nize learned over years to block out all distractions and zero in on what was most important.

This brought Nize back to the love of what she was doing and back to the time and place when she first "got it." As she practiced for each competition, her talent and countless hours of hard work, put her at the top of her game.

Nize used her vast knowledge and years of expertise to motivate her students to win competitions. The language she used may have been different at times, but the message was always the same. This had worked with her students and now she must use the same divine guidance as she prepared for the huge life-changing challenges that lay ahead of her.

Chapter Twenty-four

Nize Competes

The competition was scheduled to be held in Atlanta, Georgia, and Nize would be there to test all of her skills. She had hit the jackpot when she found her perfect model, Sue: an energetic housewife with plenty of time and a loving, understanding husband. Sue's husband wanted the best for her, but at the time, his busy work schedule did not allow him the time to accompany her on all the adventures and travels his wife desired. The job with Nize allowed her to do all the things she wanted and bring glamour to her life at the same time. Sue loved the excitement and attention of the competitions, and best of all for Nize, she had all the qualities needed in a good model. She had patience, and practice time was not a problem. Nize thought to herself, "What a find!" Sue would prove to be a good friend to Nize as well, and Sue always enjoyed the free hair services and make up lessons.

Now that she had solved that problem, Nize started to practice on Sue's hairstyle in earnest. They worked into the night many times until Nize finally sketched the style the way she thought it would look best. The style was a combination of originality and a new trend. This combination was learned from working in many student competitions. Nize knew she had a better chance of placing if the style was rhythmic, smooth, and flowing. Nize felt really good about the overall results of her hard work. Nize made Sue a long, flowing gown made of black chiffon with large ostrich feathers and a matching cape cut low in the back to show off the lines of the hairstyle.

The ballroom in Atlanta was filled with fifty beautiful models all dressed in black, with hair colored in beautiful shades of soft blonde to help the style show up better. The timekeeper yelled, "Start." Nize followed the routine she had practiced and finished in thirty-five minutes. The timekeeper yelled, "Stop," and then all the contestants quickly left the room.

The judges were thorough, and after what seemed an eternity, the third place winner was called. Nize couldn't believe it when she heard her name announced. She was both happy and sad at the same time. Nize had wanted to win first place but realized how lucky she was to have placed at all. The trophy Nize was given was large and both she and Sue were smiling wide, holding their prize high as the crowd took picture after picture.

The next competition was held in Virginia and even though the rivalry was intense, Nize walked away with a very large first place trophy. Between numerous state competitions, Nize worked very hard in both the salon and at the cosmetology college. When there was spare time, Nize practiced her skills over and over.

Eventually, Nize almost always won the competitions she entered. Her competitors were always worried when she entered the arena, but deep down Nize knew there was much more she had to do. She was focused and driven toward her goal. In order to reach the top in her chosen profession, Nize would have to continue to work hard. Nize pressed on until she had won competitions all over the US. Her next challenge would be the world Olympics, so called because it was the world championship finals of the beauty industry.

At the Olympics competition, each team would proudly enter carrying the flag of the country they represented. Because of the grand scale of the event and the many countries competing, Nize put everything she could muster into her training. The journey was very long and required discipline, determination, and lots of prayers. Nize traveled many places to learn new trends and techniques, practiced continually, and constantly thought about the Olympics competition. The practice consumed so much time and energy that Nize knew she had to have Isabel in a safe place while she fought for their financial future. Aunt Madge, Mama, and Papa happily volunteered to take good care of Isabel as Nize traveled and practiced.

Nize went to visit Isabel as often as she could but still missed her terribly. Having Aunt Madge and her parents to care for her precious daughter was a godsend, and knowing Isabel was in good hands helped Nize to continue pressing on towards her goal.

It was the longest time Nize and Isabel had been apart. In the past, Nize had been able to keep Isabel with her by taking her to the nursery and kindergarten during the day, even though she would hold back tears until she had left Isabel at the nursery, then cry all the way to work. At night Isabel and Nize would spend quality time together. Occasionally she would hire a baby sitter if she had to work late, but she always called home every few hours.

The separation was a painful time. Nize didn't trust anyone except her parents and Aunt Madge, which helped some, but guilt was always with her, unless she was with Isabel herself. She always tried to make their precious time together special. She prayed for the day when they could be together more.

Chapter Twenty-five

World's Finest

The world championships were to be held in the United States this year, instead of Europe, which would let Nize save money on travel. Nize always read all of the details of each year's championships and studied them with great scrutiny. If only she could win, it would open so many doors to a brighter future for Isabel and herself. Nize would be able to give Isabel all the things she could never afford for herself and make her Mama and Papa proud. This was Nize's motivation as she worked toward her goal. If by some miracle she could win, it would mean stardom in the beauty industry.

Nize had spent hours reading trade magazines and studying the careers of the famous stars in the business. Winning the Olympics would be the stepping stone straight to the top. Instantly the winner's face would be seen in trade magazines all over the world. It would make her an international star. However, it was a long shot for anyone because the competition drew the fiercest talent from all over the world. The competition would have many winners but only one first place for each category. The competitor scoring the most points would place first in the World Championships.

The long and difficult journey began with Nize working extra long hours in the salon, while still trying to spend as much time with Isabel as she could. Every possible minute was spent precutting and studying for the difficult task ahead. Sue, who many times had been her model, was up for the challenge. Practice sessions lasted hours as Nize worked to create the perfect hair style for Sue's bone structure that showed originality, balance, and rhythmic movement within the newest trends and competition guidelines. Nize would sometimes lie awake in the quiet of the night and create new styles and simulations for the next practice. At the next practice session she would talk it over with her trainer and they would try it out, and if it didn't work, she would go back to her mental drawing board until they had accomplished the results she needed.

Weeks and weeks passed, until Sue's hair was tired and needed to rest. Whenever this happened, Nize would work on a mannequin. It was very important to keep the model's hair healthy as long as possible. In the meantime, Nize read and studied all the hair and fashion magazines she could get her hands on. She decided to enter a state competition to sharpen her skills, but she was careful not to reveal all of her new creations, since other competitors could steal her ideas and later use them against her. Nize even kept Sue's hair covered with a scarf if she had to leave the building during a practice session.

The state competition was a big deal, but Nize felt pretty confident she would place until she saw the judges come out. There were only three of them, and they were not considered very good. Nize knew her work was very good, but when the three winners were announced, she was not one of them. She had not even received third place.

Nize went back to her room and cried as Sue did her best to comfort her. This was the first competition Nize had lost in a long time, and she was beginning to wonder if all her hard work had been in vain. After she had won so many state competitions for so long, she just couldn't understand what had happened today. What could she do now, especially since she was going to enter the world competition this year? Nize prayed for guidance as she fell sleep.

The next day Nize and Sue studied the pictures they had taken at the practice sessions. Something inside Nize seemed to say, "You know you have something special here. Don't give up now and throw it all away." After she had studied the pictures even more and worked twice as hard on the execution of the style, she began to feel better. It would be a gamble, but somehow Nize had to find out if she could be a true winner. She could not quit now because she and Sue had worked too hard. They must try again, or they would never be at peace about the competition.

Chapter Twenty-six

The Olympics

The big day arrived. It had taken weeks to prepare all the beautiful clothes Sue would wear during the competition. Nize had stayed up every night for weeks to sew the beautiful chiffon gown Sue would wear. It was a mass of chiffon and sequins from the top of the dress to the long flowing back. The white gown was what Sue and Nize had worked so hard to perfect, however the focus had to remain on emphasizing the lines and movement of the model's hair.

Nize used the look of the new American trend that season and made it her own creation by adding original touches that she carefully thought through. She diligently worked on a small hairpiece that had to quickly fit into the hairstyle and become a blended part of the total style at the time of the gala ballroom comb out. It was to be swiftly placed at the crown and had to disappear into the total design. The day style was simple but elegant, and the clothes were much more casual. The evening dress was a flowing white chiffon gown with a cape adorned with ostrich feathers and draped down the back to show the lines in the back of Sue's hair.

A cab took Nize and Sue to the hotel where they were staying for the competition, and the driver set their luggage down on the sidewalk. Suddenly, one of her large bags disappeared, and Nize saw a tall stranger dart through the revolving door. He was stealing her precious designs. Screaming at the top of her lungs, she ran after him up a large stairway and found herself in the storage area of the hotel. The man disappeared, but Nize didn't give up. She crept past all the doors until she saw shadows and light from under one of them. By then, a security guard was at the top of the stairs and Nize whispered to him, "There's someone in this room."

The guard unlocked the door, but the tall stranger darted past them and ran down the stairs. But inside the room, Nize saw a beautiful sight. The thief had opened her bag, but nothing was missing. Her gorgeous outfits for the competition were all safe.

When Nize had finally checked into her room, she opened her luggage and just stood there, touching everything. "Thank God, everything is here," she thought. She carefully hung up all the priceless gowns and accessories she had worked so hard to make and bring to New York City.

The next day, as Nize and Sue entered the large coliseum, flags from dozens of countries were being paraded around the room. The room was full of beautiful models, with precision makeup and rollers in their hair, ready to be styled and judged. Competitors from around the world were there, and Nize and Sue made their way through the large crowds to get to their dresser where Nize would do three comb-outs. When all models were seated, the Master of Ceremonies made a speech that was repeated in many languages.

Each competitor had arranged their tools in perfect order, like surgical instruments are set up in an operating room. The MC announced, "Start your day-comb," and then Nize's hands moved over Sue's head with sure and swift strokes. After fifteen minutes, the competitors left so the judges could enter and view their creations.

Six judges studied each model's head and overall appearance and scored them individually. Next came the evening comb-out competition. Sue changed into the white chiffon and lace gown with the simple, elegant neckline. Nize graced Sue's neck with a long and elegant strand of pearls. These were chosen to add more emphasis on the artistic lines of the hair design. Nize concentrated on the task at hand by blocking all distractions from her mind. Everything had to be done just like her very best practice sessions. She put the long curled eyelashes on Sue then removed the ostrich feather cape from Sue's shoulders and draped it on the back of the chair. This final touch helped create the beautiful and elegant atmosphere Nize was trying to achieve.

The MC announced that the competitors had five minutes left, just as Nize stepped back from Sue, studied the balance, arranged her pose, and blended the delicate white ornaments she had chosen for adding a touch of flowing elegance. She added the sheen of hairspray just as the time was up. The MC yelled in various languages, "Step back, do not touch your model, or you will be disqualified."

Nize looked back as she left the room and kept repeating the Lord's Prayer just as she did before each competition. The judges scored the evening styles and then left the room. It was finally time to begin the forty-five minutes for the ballroom comb-out. The dress was a mass of white billowy chiffon. The skirt flowed into a white sequined empire top with tiny straps. The sequins gave the gown a sparkling appearance that you could see all the way across the room. For the gala occasion setting, the very light and soft beige blond color of Sue's hair picked up the sparkles reflecting from the dress.

Sue could see that she looked elegant in the white sequined dress as she sat waiting for her hair to be styled. Nize took a deep breath and began. She immediately found the lines in the style with her brush. But as she reached to arrange a section of Sue's hair, she dropped her brush. Nize didn't panic and didn't waste time to pick it up. Instead, Nize reached for the spare brush she had placed on her dresser for just such an emergency. With the lines now firmly established, she followed each section with a large sharp tooth comb so not to disturb her design. She cushioned each line for a larger and more elegant ballroom style. Next, she then applied and blended a small delicate hairpiece at the crown which flowed down and into the back of the style. With that done, it became light, airy and harmonious with the entire hairstyle.

Nize quickly picked up the sheen spray and evenly misted the hairstyle with the spray to give it added brilliance and shine. Finally, she placed the sparkling diamond and pearl sequins evenly throughout the style. The total look was a magical masterpiece.

Nize was completely drained from her efforts as she left the large room. She continued to pray, flopped into a chair, closed her eyes, and waited for what seemed an eternity for the judges to finish tallying the competitor's scores.

It was finally time to return to the large room to hear the results. Nize thought, "Oh, if only I could place sixth." But her name was not called. Her fingernails cut into her palms as the MC announced the fifth place winner, which was a foreign name she'd never heard before. She watched in horror as the fourth place winner walked onto the stage, and then the third place model rose from her seat next to Sue.

"What could I have done better?" Nize asked herself. "I couldn't have worked any harder."

Second place was announced, and as "model number 10" was announced and the crowd cheered, Nize slowly walked away toward the exit. She tried to brush away the tears falling down her cheeks, but she was so disappointed that she hadn't even placed in the competition. Distantly, she heard "model number 5" called, and something told her to turn around. Sue started rising from her chair. Being so emotional, Nize didn't even realize that she was number 5. When reality finally struck her, she saw Sue desperately looking around the large room for her. As she tried to make her way to Sue, her knees nearly buckled and two good Samaritans from the audience escorted her onto the stage. Smiling widely, Nize and Sue hugged each other, and then a gold medallion on a red, white, and blue ribbon was placed around Nize's neck as the crowd cheered loudly. Nize and Sue held onto each other for a long time as the cameras flashed.

That night as she clutched the first place medallion, Nize knelt beside her bed, and whispered simply, "Thank you, thank you," over and over.

Nize was drained, but her eyes would not close. She had visions of what her reunion with Mama, Papa, Aunt Madge, and her precious Isabel would be like, and how happy they would all be. Knowing she had achieved the goal she had worked so hard for, Nize fell into a heavy sleep, smiling at the thought of sharing her joy with her family.

Chapter Twenty-seven
A Star is Born

Nize left New York and returned to her cosmetology classroom. She was sharing the good news with the admiring students when the important call came. She really didn't expect to get it so soon. It was the president of the largest beauty products company in the state.

"Congratulations, Nize," he said. "I would like you to be the guest artist for our annual convention this year," he asked. Those were truly the most beautiful words Nize could ever remember hearing.

"Finally, what I have worked so hard to achieve," Nize thought. But she knew the challenge was far from over. The convention audience must really like her, and she must prove herself on the show circuit the same way she had proved herself in the competition arena. The major difference this time would be that she would be making money instead of spending it.

Nize began to prepare in earnest for her first show since winning the Olympics. First she studied the new trends of the season, picked the best models, and designed just the right wardrobe for the presentation. Nize completed all the preparations while she continued to work in the salon and teach at the college. All of her spare time was spent preparing for the show.

The day of the convention finally arrived. Nize walked into the hotel with her head held high. The hotel and the lobby were full of cosmetologists from throughout the state. Most of them cast admiring glances as she made her way to the elevator. Nize knew she had to teach the newest and best techniques for the season, but at the same time entertain, amuse, and occasionally shock her audience in order to keep their interest.

When Nize stepped on the stage for her presentation the next morning, she felt ready. Everything, including her models and equipment, had been prepared ahead of time. As Nize looked out into the large audience she was facing, she imagined them saying, "Show me, if you can," and this honestly surprised her. She had to continuously remind herself that she had just won the world championship. "I will do this and do it well," she said to herself, as she looked out across the seemingly skeptical audience. "Good morning," Nize said in her best charming Southern accent. "I will be their friend," she thought, "and I'll treat them as I would like to be treated." The audience responded to her greeting with an enthusiastic, "Good morning."

Nize felt she was on her way now as she started her demonstration. The audience studied her thoroughly as she finished the first model, making sure they'd seen the "finished product." "I must give them something they can use when they return to their salons," she thought, as she continued to repeat each step until the audience understood how each cut would be done. Finally Nize had styled the model and then placed an ornament matching the model's outfit in her hair.

As the audience burst into applause, a lady suddenly stood and asked Nize loudly, "Do you have magic fingers?" Now this was a question that Nize had been asked many times before as she trained students for competition. When the hands of a student failed to move the hair as Nize directed them, in their frustration they would ask the same question. Nize would then gently take their hand and place hers directly over it. She would then move the hand of the curious student in the right directions and soon they were smiling. This would be the turning point in the learning process.

Nize invited the lady in the audience to come up on stage. Nize took her hand, placed her hand over the lady's, and then she felt her own hand create a beautiful movement in the model's hairstyle. A big applause erupted as the smiling lady walked off stage, however, Nize would as always, modestly explain, "My hands have had lots of practice and yes I am grateful for any talent that I may have. But study and focus, just as you are doing today and your work will become better and better. The audience had also given Nize the confidence to give her best throughout the remainder of that long day.

Model after model paraded across the stage as Nize created new and innovative styles for her audience. At the end of the day, Nize received a standing ovation as she took a bow. "I'm going to be okay," she said to herself as she looked up and quietly said again, "Thanks."

Chapter Twenty-eight

A Special Friend

As the 1960s brought change across the US, they also saw Nize's life alter in many ways. President Kennedy was shot, the Civil Rights movement took off, women across the country demanded equality, and Nize was finally the proud owner of her first beauty salon. The money to purchase the building had been borrowed from the bank, and the equipment was financed by a salon equipment company. Nize, along with her ten stylists and two assistants, were busy keeping the cash register humming.

Many clients passed through the tastefully designed front door of the salon but one stood out in Nize's heart and mind forever. Mrs. Mary, as Nize affectionately called her, was pleasingly plump and had dark brown hair. She continuously needed perms, color, and lots of teasing to keep the French twist and mass of curls on top of her head looking neat. Nize made Mrs. Mary very happy each week as she sat in her styling chair. The two of them had communicated well from the first day Mrs. Mary came to the salon. It was a professional friendship as they discussed world events and personal histories. Nize always listened to Mrs. Mary's opinion as her hands swiftly worked the woman's hair into the exact style she requested.

Mrs. Mary was a very intelligent woman who was a retired nurse. When she was young, she had met and married a doctor from the hospital where she worked. Later, Mrs. Mary's husband opened up his own medical practice, and she worked side by side with him for many years. Together they made many good financial decisions, which resulted in financial independence for them. It was not obvious that they had acquired a great deal of wealth because Mrs. Mary enjoyed the simpler things in life and never flaunted her money.

She was always jolly and pleasant until the day she sat in Nize's salon dressed in mourning attire. Nize quietly styled Mrs. Mary's hair in preparation for her husband's funeral. She explained how much of a shock it had been when a brain aneurysm had taken him without warning. Nize tried to comfort her by mentioning he didn't suffer when he died. "That's something to be grateful for," Nize whispered to her client. Mrs. Mary was trying very hard to be brave as she nodded her head in sad agreement. However, in the weeks that followed Mrs. Mary was quiet and depressed. Each week Nize spent some extra time trying to cheer her up as best she could. Slowly, Mrs. Mary started to talk more as Nize patiently listened to her.

One afternoon, something happened in the salon that seemed to bring her back more than anything. "Call an ambulance!" screamed one of the stylists. One of the assistants had apparently begun choking on an aspirin and was lying on the floor with the frantic stylists surrounding her. The woman was turning blue when suddenly Mrs. Mary had her short, plump arms around her. With closed fists, she went for the diaphragm while performing the Heimlich maneuver. The aspirin went sailing through the air and landed on a counter across the room. Without saying a word, Mrs. Mary sat down back into Nize's chair as all the clients in the crowded salon applauded her life-saving efforts. This was a turning point in Mrs. Mary's grieving process.

Whenever Nize had to leave town to teach or attend classes, Mrs. Mary would always slip money into her pocket. Each time Nize found the bills she always knew who had put it there. Mrs. Mary had learned from others how Nize had been struggling financially for a long time, though Nize had never complained to anyone about her situation.

As she continued to work three jobs, Nize kept praying someday she could afford a real house for herself and Isabel. But expenses kept piling up. Her traveling jobs were taking more and more time, and she barely had time for her regular customers, including Mrs. Mary. In order for the business to succeed, she hired a manager to run the shop.

One day when Nize retuned home she found a letter from the bank as she looked through a large stack of unopened mail. It requested Nize come to the bank to claim a check. Tears streamed down Nize's face as the banker informed her that Mrs. Mary had died some time ago and had remembered her in her will. The fact that Mrs. Mary felt that Nize was so special was overwhelming to Nize.

After she left the bank, Nize found the cemetery where Mrs. Mary had been buried. Nize sat at her grave for a long time and talked to her just as they used to when she was styling Mrs. Mary's hair. It made Nize feel good to know that someone with whom she had a professional relationship with for so many years could have turned out to be so special. It was not a lot of money, but it was good to know that you had meant so much to someone's life.

Things were improving financially for Nize. She was saving money to buy that special house for her and Isabel, so that someday she could afford to take more time off to be with her daughter. She knew that it was crucial to stay in the spotlight a little longer. Show business was that way. A star had to work hard while the publicity was there and her name was still well-known. Isabel traveled with Nize often now. She loved watching the models, but Nize could only take her when Sue or someone would help keep her safe. Isabel was becoming travel-smart, as she knew her way around hotels and restaurants. Isabel was a busy girl, and Nize made sure to teach her to be independent for her own safety in life.

Chapter Twenty-nine

Scary Trip to Chicago

Sam was one of Nize's best salon managers, so he would be traveling to Chicago with Nize to the large Midwest show. Nize and Sam had a platonic relationship, and Sam would protect her from any undesirable male admirers when he was around. They both enjoyed the glamour of their profession and worked well together.

Nize, Sam, and some of the other employees checked into adjoining rooms at the Palmer Hotel when they reached Chicago. Nize needed solitude to think and rest until her major work for the show was finished. Tonight she had agreed to help a colleague with some tutoring for a competition the next day. Everyone gathered in Nize's suite to watch, and after several hours the room had become quite stuffy. It was getting late and since no one was in the halls this time of night, they decided to open the door to the hallway.

Everyone was enjoying an artistic evening when out of nowhere, an angry hotel attendant was standing in the doorway to Nize's room. "Don't you people know there has been a murder here?" he asked. "Close your door so everyone can be safe," he demanded. He explained how the murderer was still on the loose. The door was quickly closed as everyone in the room stood in shock and wondered what they should do. No one in Nize's room wanted to leave.

Morning came and everyone was still huddled together in Nize's room. No one left the room until Nize called the front desk and was informed by hotel staff that the murderer had been found early that morning.

Nize planned on catching up on her sleep on the plane as she had done many times before. Unfortunately, she would not get the luxury this time. Nize and Sam had barely dosed off when suddenly, there was a jolt which nearly knocked both of them from their seats. It seemed the plane had dropped several feet. Both of them sat up and looked at each other with wide eyes, wondering what was happening. Just then, the lights in the plane's cabin started to flicker.

The flight was close to landing when every light in the cabin went out, leaving the passengers in total darkness. It was so quiet you could hear a pin drop. No one spoke. Nize calmly sat in her seat and prayed. Minutes went by in silence as they felt the distinct sense of descending. The plane landed safely and the lights came on again. Sam looked over at Nize and loudly declared, "I will never ever fly again!" When he finally got off the plane, Sam bent down and thankfully kissed the ground.

Even though the last few minutes had been frightening, Nize couldn't help chuckling to herself. She knew Sam would fly again just as she would in a few days to go on an assignment in Hawaii. Despite some turbulence in her life, things were looking up for Nize.

Chapter Thirty

Brief Encounter

Nize traveled all the way to Hawaii to do a show. It was the end of the first day and all the guest artists were expected to attend the dance in the evening so the audience would have a chance to meet them personally. Nize wore a soft pink gown with a matching turban studded with rhinestones. She was escorted into the ballroom on the arm of her employer. He was a stately man who had obtained great wealth in the beauty business. Nize was his prize—both an asset to his company and something of a mascot. Nize had headlined all of his big conventions and was the company's trademark. If any cosmetologist had questions about anything in the business, Nize was there to answer them. Her boss had come to understand and respect Nize.

"Nize," her boss said, "there are some very important people here tonight. That good-looking fellow walking over here is the president of the largest hair care manufacturing company in the world." The two business tycoons met face-to-face and warmly shook hands. "Meet the best guest artist around," Nize's boss said as he presented her.

"Yes, I know," the handsome stranger replied, "and she is also the prettiest." He smiled at her. "May I have this dance?" The man's good looks were surpassed only by his ability to gracefully glide across the dance floor.

"I would love to show you around the island," he said. "We can break out of here, and explore with some people from my company," he explained.

"Why not," Nize thought since she had finished her show and would be leaving Hawaii tomorrow. It would be nice to see a little more of Hawaii, since her schedule didn't usually allow much time for sightseeing. Nize joined her host and the others on a long white yacht with breathtaking views of the island at night. Later, limousines took them to the most elite nightclubs where she enjoyed a wonderful evening filled with dancing, good conversation, and lots of laughter. By the time they returned to the hotel, it was the wee hours of the morning. Everyone had gone to their rooms as Nize stood by her host in the lobby of the hotel.

"Come up to my room for a nightcap," he suggested to Nize.

"Think of something quick," Nize thought to herself and then said, "I'm so sorry but I have a really bad headache."

"I have aspirin," he said.

Nize politely replied, "Thank you for a wonderful evening, but I can't go to your room."

The man angrily walked away, without saying another word to Nize. The handsome businessman did not speak when Nize passed him in the hotel lobby the next morning either. Nize ran into her boss and one of his male employees. They were both wearing wide grins, which puzzled Nize. The two men began to laugh loudly at Nize. "Tell her what you did," the boss said.

"Thank you for not letting me down," the employee told her.

"What do you mean?" Nize asked.

"They had a bet on you," the boss replied.

"You mean he thought he could add me to his collection of conquests?" Nize asked.

"Sorry," chuckled the employee.

Nize walked away shaking her head. "Men," she said under her breath as she continued walking. "Female guest artists have many challenges," Nize thought. "I intend to meet them one by one and survive in this business. God help me, I will prevail."

Chapter Thirty-one

The Message

The show in Hawaii had been a huge success, and Nize was pleased with the response from her audience. However, as she sat alone on the plane that would take her to her next assignment, she couldn't stop thinking about the bet the guys had made about her. Would she or wouldn't she sleep with the idol from the cosmetic company? "What a rotten bet to make," she thought. She had shrugged it off in Hawaii and pretended it hadn't bothered her, but the truth be told it had bothered her a great deal. It made her feel angry as though she was fighting against the big uncertain world all alone. This was not the first challenge she had faced being a traveling career woman, nor would it be the last. She had been especially vulnerable since becoming a successful and well-known businesswoman. Some male co-workers had continually challenged her talents as well as her morals. She prayed, "Please make me strong, Lord, and don't let me fall," before drifting off to sleep with a very heavy heart.

Suddenly from out of nowhere came a strong and very soothing voice. "You will be sent a helpmate," the voice said.

Even in her slumber Nize asked, "How will I know him?"

"It will be as clear as a bell to you," the voice answered.

Nize would be truly grateful for some help in her life, so she asked, "What should I do for you?"

"Love him," the soothing voice answered, and it was silent.

Nize was shaking as she sat up in her seat. The voice had seemed so real to her. Nize looked around the plane and desperately wanted to stand up and tell everyone what had just happened to her, but she stopped, because she was sure no one would believe her. "They're only human," she thought, "but at the same time I must tell someone when the time is right. I'm sure the voice was real and what I heard will happen. I know this as much as I know I'm alive," Nize thought.

Throughout the remainder of the flight Nize sat in her seat and stared into space with tears of happiness in her eyes and a lump in her throat. She had never felt as much love as she felt right then, and she felt content.

She met some nice men, after that, and even went on a few dates, but it would be some time before the message she heard on the plane trip from Hawaii was confirmed. Nize never worried about being alone after that day, though. She knew, in her head and her heart, when the time was right, there would be a helpmate for her, and there was no need to worry about it. Nize continued to be confident and content in her present life and knew that God had plans for her future.

Chapter Thirty-two

Judging

One of Nize's responsibilities as a guest lecturer at cosmetology conventions was to judge competitions. There were many types of competitions at each convention—haircutting, styling, day, evening, ballroom, gala, and creative. The most elaborate of the competitions was the Parade of Affiliates. This fanciful competition was serious business, and people were sent in to examine each model prior to the judging to make sure no cheating occurred. For example, in haircutting, if there were only a few pieces of hair left on the floor it was assumed an expert had precut it before the judging commenced. In styling, the models were examined to see if there had been pre-setting or loosening of the set before the comb-out. After the examination of the models was complete, the judges were announced and the judge's credentials read – they proudly entered the room. Nize's accomplishments in cosmetology competitions were unsurpassed and competitors where happy when she made her entrance into the room. She was always greeted with much applause, but on this particular night in Atlanta, she was challenged.

Nize had completed her lectures and was about to enter a room full of models from all across Georgia to judge the Parade of Affiliates. The coastal district sent a beautiful mermaid with a long and glittery tail. The peanut farms area had sent a gorgeous model dressed as a peanut.

The very large room was filled with beautiful representatives, and everyone wanted to win and be sent to the national competition. All six judges circled each model again as they labored over their decisions, and finally Nize had picked three winners.

Third place was a stunning blonde model with a large satin bowl attached to her waistline filled with large plastic, peach halves, and her makeup was frosted peach to match.

Second place was a tall redhead wearing a form-fitting gold gown with a matching cape, which made the outfit seem like a large trophy. She was also holding a large trophy and had a banner across her shoulders with the words, "Atlanta Trophy Winner" in glitter. This representation alluded to the fact Atlanta had won so many trophies in the beauty business.

She gave first place to a model, representing the University of Georgia, dressed in school colors with a red velvet body suit, black net stockings and an abbreviated black graduation gown with a matching mortar board. Her beautiful black hairstyle had a sprayed-in light gray streak, which represented too much studying or extracurricular activities (according to the description read aloud). This model's young son was dressed like the Georgia Bulldog, Uga. Uga's paper maché mask was very convincing as was his mother's graduation gown and the message was intellectually humorous.

Backstage when the tallying was completed there was a tie, and Nize's first had to be judged again. After all the judges were sent back in Nize began to worry if she had been wrong. She had studied the total over and over again as she looked at the University of Georgia representation. But she could not change her score as all of her intellect told her she had to go with her first score. Tally workers backstage added the scores as Nize stood firm and waited. This was the hard part of judging since sometimes a personal favorite might be passed over for the majority vote. The scores were tallied, and the winners were presented on a large revolving stage so the two thousand cosmetologists in the audience could see them.

Nize could barely see the stage from the judges' room but as the third place winner walked off the stage and onto the runway she saw a bowl of peaches. Then the crowd applauded as the "trophy from Atlanta" received the second place trophy. The crowd went wild as the first place trophy was presented to the mother and son while the band played the University of Georgia's fight song.

Nize knew the decision was unanimous and her first place winner had been the right decision. She was happy for the model and her young son. Nize had been afraid they had touched her heart and she had not used her professional judgment which was always the first priority. She knew one must always first go by the rules of the competition but somehow this night was special. She had gone by the rules because this was truly the best work in the categories. Nize was relieved by the results but her heart was especially happy for the young boy who would always remember this night. Nize left the room with a very large smile on her face. It had been an especially good day to be a judge!

Chapter Thirty-three

The Attraction

Nize was teaching at the National Convention in Washington, D.C. and staying in a nice hotel. Most times after doing a show she ate in her room, but tonight she needed to be around people. She really missed Isabel and didn't feel like being alone, so she ate in the hotel dining room. A waiter came to her table and politely said, "Miss, the gentleman across the room asked me to bring this bottle of our best wine to your table," as he handed her a note. It read:

I would love to join you for a drink if you would be kind enough to allow me to do so. If not, please enjoy the wine.

~Senator Mike from Pennsylvania.

The waiter pointed to the handsome stranger across the room. He nodded his head and smiled at Nize. The waiter added, "He comes here often."

"And is this a frequent pattern of his?" Nize asked. "Does he always send bottles of wine to women?"

"No, Miss," the waiter replied. "This is a first. He is usually having meetings with other politicians."

"Tell the gentleman he may join me," Nize instructed the waiter. The senator had a very striking resemblance to Al Pacino and was just as charming. The ensuing conversation came easily since they had so much in common with all the traveling they each did. Nize and Mike discussed good and bad hotels, interesting foods, and the shared woe of delayed flights. Good Italian food was Mike's favorite. His grandparents had come to the United States from Palermo, and he grew up eating lots of pasta. Nize was truly enjoying her dinner companion's company and accepted his invitation for lunch the next day.

Nize and Mike shared a lovely lunch outside a quaint restaurant. It was spring-time, and the fragrance of cherry blossoms wafted through the air as they walked back to the hotel. "Could I see you again sometime soon?" he asked Nize in the hotel lobby.

"I'm doing a show in Hershey in two weeks," Nize replied.

"It's a date, then," he said with a big smile. Nize enjoyed his company, but at the same time he made her a little nervous.

Nize had settled into her assignment at the Convention Center in Hershey a couple of weeks later where the aroma of chocolate floated in the air. Everyone at the show had been so nice, and the audience seemed spellbound by her rich Southern accent.

That same evening, Mike arrived in a bright red Cadillac convertible. "I have some people I would like you to meet," he said as they drove to the country. He stopped at a large beautiful country house with a beautiful lawn. "Meet my parents," Mike said. Nize was never so shocked or flattered as when Mike introduced her to every one of his relatives. They enjoyed a backyard barbecue followed by music and dancing.

Nize was attracted to Mike, but her heart was telling her everything was moving way too fast, especially since the memory of Andy had never really been far from her thoughts or heart. "I'm not sure I'm ready for this," she thought as they drove back to town. Mike kissed Nize passionately as they walked to her room at the hotel. "When will I see you again?" he asked.

"Mike, I'm sorry but I have a confession," Nize painfully told Mike. "This has been so lovely and I like you so much, but..." Nize said. She couldn't bring herself to tell him about Isabel – an illegitimate child would not fit into his "career".

Mike interrupted her by saying "But what?"

"But I just can't do this right now," Nize confessed. "It's moving too fast. Maybe you could give me more time and perhaps in the future – just not now," Nize said sadly.
Mike looked hurt, but how could she explain to him how she felt? She had places to go and goals she wanted to achieve, and she couldn't just stop now when she was a career woman with a child. Isabel had to come first in her life. The promises she had made to herself so many times to make a future for Isabel kept going through her mind because she owed her precious daughter that much.

"Will we meet again?" Mike sadly asked.

As she walked into her room, Nize turned back and smiled at him. "You bet!"

Chapter Thirty-four

Fame

Nize would headline this year's International Beauty Show in New York City as the guest artist. Thousands of people from all over the world paid lots of money for tickets to the show. It was like a Broadway production, and even had dancers as a backup for Nize's presentations. Music from The Great Gatsby movie played, and modern versions of 1930's outfits were worn by the models and dancers. Nize performed her magic on the models' hair while she showed her audience the newest trends and techniques in hairstyling. Nize's own wardrobe for the show was part of the glamour of the international event.

Nize's informative presentations thrilled her audiences and the "how to books" she wrote sold out early on the first day of the show. Students stood in line to register for advanced classes to be held at the cosmetology college where Nize taught. Nize had "arrived" and was living the life for which she had long dreamed. It was more exciting than she ever imagined.

The next day, Nize arrived early to make sure everything was ready for her presentations, and she discovered one of her models was missing. She had suspected the young man would not show up, as he had done a few times in the past. She quickly rearranged the model line up so the show could go on as scheduled. Nize always made sure her audiences were entertained, and, show after show, she never let her spectators down. Usually she received standing ovations.

Finally the show was over and Nize was sitting in her dressing room with her eyes closed – both exhausted and relieved. There was a knock on her door, and she thought perhaps it was one of the stagehands who she wished would just go away. The knocking became louder and louder, and finally she rose to answer it. She was not at all prepared for what happened when she reluctantly opened the door. There stood a tall, blonde man with beautiful blue eyes she had never forgotten. "Nize," he said.

"Andy?" she quietly asked the man.

"Yes," he answered. They stood there, staring at each other, neither capable of uttering a sound. Andy said, "I saw you on television, and I had to see you."

"It's been such a long time," Nize said softly.

"There are so many things I need to tell you. I hope you'll have dinner with me and let me explain," Andy asked.

"Come to my hotel at seven tonight."

He nodded. "I'll see you then," he said, and walked away.

Nize put her hands over her mouth to keep from screaming since her emotions were so strong. She quickly opened the bottle of sherry her assistant left for her to celebrate with at the end of the show, and took a long swig.

Nize was in the tub, back at her hotel, when the phone rang. She thought it would stop ringing after a while, so she continued to enjoy her soothing bath. But it didn't stop, so Nize got out and answered it.

It was Aunt Madge. In a trembling voice, she said, "I'm so sorry, Nize, but there was an accident and Isabel was in the car. It's bad, Nize. She's on her way to the emergency room right now."

In shock, Nize hung up and quickly dialed the airport. The voice at the other end of the phone informed her she could get a direct flight to Myrtle Beach, if she could hurry to the airport. She barely made the flight, and on the whole way back to the beach she sat with her head bowed. She kept saying over and over again, "Forgive me for being such a bad mother. Please give me another chance to make it up to my precious Isabel. I'll give up my career and be the best mother. Please let Isabel live. Please."

Finally the plane landed and Nize made it to the hospital just as Isabel was being taken into the operating room by hospital staff.

Chapter Thirty-five

The Gift

Nize impatiently waited for news in the hospital's waiting room. As she sat there alone, her mind went back to the early part of her career. Though she knew it was illogical, she thought perhaps if only she had spent more time with Isabel, maybe this wouldn't have happened. What could she have done differently to make their lives better? Nize could not stop the tears running down her cheeks, no matter how much she tried to think positive thoughts. After a while she didn't even try.

Suddenly, two familiar figures stood before Nize and were a most welcome sight. It had been such a long time since she had seen her parents, and now they were here for her when she needed them. Nize quickly got up and the three of them hugged for a long time without saying anything. They sat in silence in the waiting room chairs. "I did lots of things wrong," Nize began telling her parents. "If only I had been with Isabel more, maybe she wouldn't be in surgery right now. I only wish I could go back in time. If only I could change everything I did wrong," she sighed.

Mama rose slowly from her chair and stood before Nize. "Look at me," she said. "I should have told you this a long time ago.

"When you were very young I knew you were different. It bothered me until the day I watched as you took the poor little girl with a dirty face into your bedroom. After a while, she came out completely transformed into a beautiful child. I almost didn't recognize her. Her hair was different, her outfit was one you had picked out from your own clothes, and in her hair were some of you favorite ribbons. You had turned her into Cinderella, and when she saw her reflection in the mirror, she was the happiest little girl in the world. I knew then why you were different. You had a gift from God, and since God created so much beauty in this world for us to enjoy, he needed some help here on earth to help his favored creatures become even more beautiful.

"So you see Nize, it was your duty to use it and remember God never punishes us for using the gifts with which he blessed us. You have helped so many people in ways you could never imagine, so be thankful for your teaching ability. It has helped many people to make a better life for themselves."

Nize thought about what her mother had just said and stood up and held onto her. In her heart, Nize knew her mother, who was a woman of few words, had spoken the kindest speech Nize had ever heard.

They saw the doctor walking toward them, and they all froze. Nize tried to prepare herself mentally for the news about the surgery. "The surgery went well," the doctor happily told them, "but your daughter will still need lots of rest in order to make a full and complete recovery."

Papa stood up and all three of them hugged each other and laughed with joy. "God is so good," Papa said and Nize and Mama nodded in agreement with him.

Chapter Thirty-six

A Daughter

Andy had endured his last surgery and the operation had been successful—he would walk with only a slight limp. He had completed his residency in a prestigious New York hospital and was well on his way to a successful career in medicine. Now he could think about seeing Nize again.

He went back to see the old doctor so he could try to get some information about her. The old doctor immediately recognized Andy because he had admired his work as an intern. But when the doctor was asked about the pretty student Andy was so smitten over at the college infirmary, the older man said he couldn't remember. Finally, he said he thought he remembered something about her getting a blood test so she could get married. In his own mind, the old doctor was trying to keep Andy from getting a broken heart by chasing after a girl who had messed up her own life.

Andy left the old doctor shocked, disappointed, and puzzled. No one else could tell him where Nize lived. Andy went back to his work but he did not give up his search for Nize. Andy thought the doctor's memory was probably not very accurate so he went on with his life. But he still thought about Nize every day.

One night, years later, while watching the news, Andy saw a story about the International Convention for Cosmetologists that featured Nize. She was even more beautiful than he remembered. The newscaster told about her many fans and how many people had come to the convention that day just to watch her teach and perform. Andy, overcome with joy, decided he would go see Nize the next day after her performance.

Andy reminisced about Nize as he watched the news broadcast. Though they hadn't known each other that long, he knew he had truly been in love with her. The reason his other relationships had never worked out was because he never found anyone who could replace Nize in his heart. Now he could see her and find some answers at last. He hoped she had not married, but if she had, he would walk away because he still loved her.

The next day he went to the convention, found Nize's dressing room, and knocked on the door. Finally facing her, he wanted to say so many things but she wanted to talk in her hotel room later that evening.

When Andy knocked on Nize's hotel room door that evening, the person who answered the door wasn't Nize, but a pretty model-type who politely said, "May I help you?"

"I'm an old friend of Nize's, and she's having dinner with me tonight," Andy replied.

"I'm Sue, one of Nize's models. But she isn't here because her daughter was in a really bad car accident," she replied.

"Was her husband with her daughter?" Andy asked the model before he could help himself.

"Oh no, Nize had never married," Sue replied.

Andy felt tremendous relief go through his body. He couldn't help but stare at a large picture sitting on the desk of a child who looked to be about eight years old. There was something familiar about her eyes and Andy picked up the picture to study it.

"She's beautiful, isn't she?" Sue asked Andy. "Nize says she has her father's eyes." Suddenly Andy was excusing himself and trying hard to understand everything that had happened to him since he first saw Nize today.

Once he was outside the hotel, Andy decided to visit the old doctor once more, because something didn't add up. He drove south for hours and was finally shaking hands with his medical mentor again. "I'm here for some help," Andy pleaded to the doctor. "I once asked you about Nize, the student I had a crush on when I interned with you. I don't know if you knew that we saw each other after I met her in the college infirmary."

The old doctor looked very surprised. "Sometimes it's better to let things be," he said.

"She has a daughter," Andy told the doctor. Now the doctor acted as if he wanted to cooperate. He slowly nodded, "Yes."

"Where?" asked Andy.

"I sent her to a good hospital. I'll make a call," he told Andy while reaching for the phone. "You'll have to go pick up the birth certificate yourself," the doctor told him.

Andy immediately left the doctor and was in his car, headed to the hospital. Since he was expected, it didn't take long for the attendant to reach into a file cabinet and give him a birth certificate. The answer to Andy's question was at the bottom of the document—his full name was spelled out on the line that indicated he was Isabel's father.

Andy was in a daze as he drove to Myrtle Beach. "I must see her," he thought. If only he had known the truth. He wondered why Nize didn't try to find him. He knew he had disappeared for a long time recuperating from his injuries, so maybe she had tried and couldn't find him. Maybe she thought he didn't want her. He knew he had to make everything right.

It was morning by the time he reached Myrtle Beach Hospital, and he could only find out Isabel had been discharged. No one knew where she was going, and no one answered the phone numbers they had given hospital staff.

Andy remembered the hotel owned by Nize's Aunt Madge. The front desk attendant gave him all the information he needed. Andy vowed to himself he'd never lose Nize or Isabel again, so there was no time to waste. He began to take some drastic steps to accomplish his mission!

Chapter Thirty-seven

The Surprise

Nize stood beside Isabel's bed for a long time, and then her precious daughter opened her eyes, looked up at her mother, and smiled bravely. "I'm going to stay with you," Nize softly said to Isabel. The little girl fell asleep again while Nize sat in the large chair beside her bed. Hours passed, and as she dozed on and off, she thought about her and Isabel's future. Nize knew she had to find a way to be able to spend more time with her daughter.

Nize opened her eyes to see Isabel, who was now wide awake, reach for her. Nize held her close and whispered, "You're going to be okay. I'll buy that beach house on Pleasure Island, and we'll have a long, wonderful holiday. Just as soon as you can leave, we'll be on our way." A tiny tear of happiness rolled down Isabel's cheek as she held her mother's hand.

"Thanks," Isabel whispered, then she went back to sleep with a contented look on her face. Nize went outside for some fresh air, hoping it would help to keep her awake.

The next morning was very beautiful especially since Isabel was out of danger. Nize called the real estate agent she had been in touch with and immediately purchased the house on Pleasure Island they had looked at months before. Pleasure Island's beaches possessed a family atmosphere that she'd longed for. Nize knew her life was almost back on track, but she had to deal with the terrible disappointment of losing Andy once again.

Nize imagined him going to the hotel to see her, only to find her gone. She tried to imagine what he thought – probably that she had played a cruel joke on him. It was difficult to think about his expression when the hotel staff told him she had left quickly and they had no idea where she went. She was afraid Andy would give up forever this time and never get to know his beautiful daughter. She really had no way of knowing where to find him or if he would ever want to see her again. She also wondered if the old doctor had told him anything about Isabel, and if he had, how he felt about her.

All these emotions overwhelmed her, so she sat down on the sidewalk and bowed her head. An elderly lady tapped her on her shoulder and asked if she was alright. Nize shook her head and said, "I'll be fine." She stood up and walked back to Isabel's room.

After Isabel was released from the hospital, she and Nize picked up Aunt Madge, and the three of them drove through Southport to the ferry that would take them to their new house on Pleasure Island. It was a beautiful day as they floated down the Cape Fear River. Nize had always loved going across on the ferry to the island because the trip was so peaceful. She was happy to be able to spend time with Isabel and Aunt Madge, but there was a wound in her heart because of how close she had come to finding Andy again. But she had been through pain before. Feeling the breeze on her skin and watching the clouds floating above her in the sky, she knew she had a friend who would always comfort and take care of her.

Suddenly Nize heard a very loud noise coming from overhead. She looked up, trying hard to focus through the bright sunlight, and realized it was a helicopter coming closer and closer. What could possibly be wrong, she wondered. Could they be in some sort of danger, and someone was trying to warn the crew?

Something was thrown from the helicopter and it landed at Nize's feet. She reluctantly reached down and picked up the box. She peeked through a crack in the lid and saw a lady's golf glove. Immediately she knew what was happening; Andy was in the helicopter! He was so close she could see him laughing, and suddenly she was laughing too. The helicopter lifted up and away from the ferry and made its way to the shore for a dry landing spot. Nize's eyes followed it while it landed, and she kept remembering the message she had once received while returning on a plane from Hawaii, "You will receive a helpmate."

There was no doubt in her mind about the message.
It was now, "as clear as a bell!"

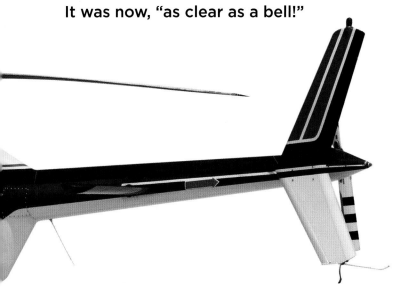

The Author

While "Nize" is a work of fiction it was created by the author, Esther Myles, based on her rich life and career in the Beauty Industry. She wanted to create a story that would inspire young people to seek their path in this multi-billion dollar industry that is filled with opportunities. In writing the book, Esther has drawn from some of her memorable experiences and added much from her creative imagination, however, this is a work of fiction, and should not be interpreted as portraying any actual persons or events.

She has dedicated the book to the memory of her parents. They raised her in rural North Carolina without the luxuries we enjoy today but with a love that she will never forget. Unlike many children today Esther did not suffer through a broken home life, abuse, alcoholic parents, financial ruin or domestic arguments. Her formative years occurred in a loving family setting – where family values came first. Esther credits much of her success and happiness in life to this upbringing.

Life on the farm was rough and dirty work, however, and Esther, being drawn to the glamorous and beautiful side of things, was eager to see the bright lights of the big city. She made her way to New York City at seventeen and life was never the same. It took several years before she enrolled in Beauty School and once there she knew she had found her calling. She fell in love with the education, techniques, customers, variety, glamour and excitement she experienced every day in the School and her enthusiasm and talent brought her quick recognition.

Her schooling began in one of the premier regional schools, Troutman's College of Hairstyling in Wilmington, NC. There she was exposed to the best instructors and moral conduct of the time. This was a time of starched white uniforms, well shined shoes, punctual appointments and the recital of the Lord's Prayer every morning before class. Later in her career she became an Instructor, Competition Trainer and Styles Director for Charles Troutman, son of the school founders, in Raleigh, NC, and authored a book of hair styling for his school. The Troutman's were a credit to the industry and a great influence on a young girl embarking on a new career. Esther never forgot the many lessons learned from this family who "practiced what they preached".

After graduation Esther quickly began to find recognition and success when she took her first job as stylist for a large department store in Raleigh, the state capital of North Carolina. She had done so well the first few days that she was shortly promoted to Head Stylist of the salon. Customers were soon showing up from all over the state for Esther's special touch.

Esther then moved to Athens, Georgia while her husband attended Veterinarian Medical College and she quickly established her credentials and reputation for working miracles with her "magic fingers" on her many customers. It was in Georgia that she first entered into the competition arena, winning in her first competition. Being close to Atlanta, where regional and national competitions and conventions were held, she was exposed to greats like; Jamison Shaw, Olympics Champion; Leo Passage, founder Pivot Point International, Inc.; platform artists like Styles Adamson & Brothers, Rita Clayburn and many other inspiring talents.

She continued to improve her talents and exposure by attending advanced classes, cosmetology conventions and entering competitions. She and other affiliate members of the Athens, Georgia chapter of the NCA took another first place for the State when she helped design and modeled a University of Georgia "coed" theme and convinced her young son to accompany her on stage for the competition as Uga, the University bulldog mascot.

The thrill of competing and winning never grew old with Esther and she would pour all her energy and talent into every competition, both as participant and later as a coach and trainer, as she taught others the skills necessary to become champions. She later achieved regional fame as Instructor and Trainer as her students won over 200 trophies, often sweeping the top three places in competition. She then received national and international recognition after two successful trips as Trainer, with different student teams, to the International Beauty Show in New York and returning with the "World's Supreme Student Hair Styling Contest" Championship Trophy in 1968 and then again in 1969. This brought Esther more offers and opportunities including the chance to be a "platform artist" and "star" performer at industry shows and conventions around the country for national companies such as Loreal, Conair, Clairol, Redken and others. She was also Guest Artist for 18 years for B&H, the leading distributor of beauty products in North Carolina and taught many advanced private workshops to other instructors.

Her Guest Artist appearances brought her into contact with many "stars" of the industry such as Vidal Sasson. She also was exposed to many personalities in the entertainment/political world such as Bob Denver "Gilligan" (coloring his hair in her Raleigh salon), Priscilla Pressley (designing a hairstyle Priscilla wanted to adopt) and President Gerald Ford (sitting next to him during an awards presentation and enjoying an engaging conversation). She and her students also worked on the "Hudsucker Proxy" in Wilmington, NC, starring Paul Newman, Jennifer Jason Lee and Tim Robbins.

In 1981, Esther returned to her roots in eastern North Carolina and convinced the local community college President that he needed to open a cosmetology school as part of his curriculum. This began a new chapter in her life as she reestablished herself close to her aging parents and trained many new students while building a thriving school business for the college. She was named "Teacher of the Year", in 1986, for Brunswick Community College under the statewide "Awards for Excellence in Teaching" program established by the State Board of Community Colleges. Then, in 1989, she received the North Carolina, "Joe Snoutherly Teacher of the Year" award from the North Carolina State Board of Cosmetic Art Examiners.

Esther is grateful for all God's blessing in her life and is quick to give Him credit for all of her good decisions and success. "Nize's" faith, prayers and spiritual experiences draw from many actual "experiences of faith" in Esther's life. She plans several other books as time goes on to emphasize this. One of the overwhelming experiences of Esther's life, after her divorce, was God's hand in bringing her a "helpmate" some 22 years ago. They are happily married with three children-stepchildren and five grandchildren between them and she credits her "helpmate's" influence and help with bringing this book to press. She has tried to bring some of that "magic" to life in this story of "Nize" as she wants to tell all of God's promise to help those who will work and pray to find their way in this difficult but exciting life we are privileged to live.

Early Years

Esther wins first competition she enters.

Esther wins 1st place in fifth district of Georgia.

Esther and son win 1st place trophy in Atlanta.

Nize - The Making of a Champion

1968

International Competition New York 1968 & 1969

Esther, as trainer, leads students to 1st and 3rd place trophies in 1968 and 1st place in 1969 in World's Supreme Student Hairstyling Competitions.

1969

E TO THE '69 International Beauty Show
GOLDEN 50TH JUBILEE

1986 Brunswick Community College
Teacher of the Year

Courtesy of
The Brunswick Beacon

Esther as Coach
& Trainer

Esther breaking
ground at BCC's
new expansion

1989 North Carolina
Cosmetology
Teacher of the Year

Friends & Family

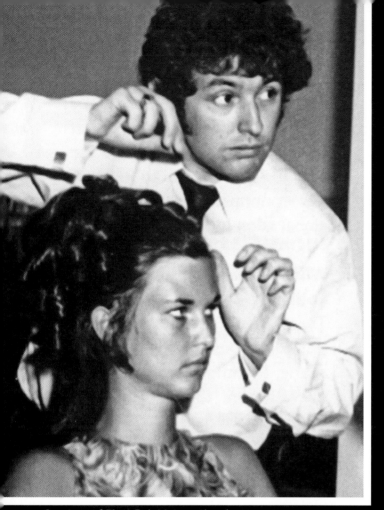

excellence

PIVOT POINT®

Leo
PASSAGE

Esther Myles first saw Leo Passage in the early-60's in Atlanta Georgia where he was participating in a competition. She was new to the business and attending the Beauty Convention to further her education. She recognized a tremendous talent and skill though both she and Leo were young and untested. Later Esther began to hear more and more about his rising stature in the industry, both as a competitor and instructor.

Three or four years later, Esther, now teaching cosmetology, learned the basic Pivot Point System as part of her advanced education. As she began to train students in competition, she was able to take advanced training classes from Leo himself, in Chicago, at his Pivot Point School. She found this training invaluable when she returned to the competition arena as a Trainer. She became a lifelong advocate of Leo's Pivot Point Program.

Esther credits Leo's training and scientific approach to hair design with raising her competition skills to a new level, and in her words, "changed her professional life to one of a champion trainer". It was not long after this that she took her students to the 1968 International Beauty Show in New York. They returned home with the first and second place trophies in "The World's Supreme Student Styling Competition". Returning in 1969 with a different team of students, they earned the first place trophy again.

Later in her career as Lead Instructor at Brunswick Community College she instituted the Pivot Point Program in her curriculum with superior results for her students. She considers Leo Passage a giant in the industry and her favorite mentor. She encourages all those who wish to improve their skills and understanding of this exciting industry to consider becoming versed in the Pivot Point System.

Leo Passage, Founder of Pivot Point International, Inc., was recently honored at the 3rd Annual International Legends Ball for his lifetime of outstanding contributions to the highest standards of the professional salon industry. He is credited with changing the concepts behind cosmetology education by shattering the myth that successful designers must be born with artistic ability. His "scientific approach" to cosmetology is rooted in the Bauhaus Theory and based on a unique harmony between science, technology and art. In 1962, he founded Pivot Point International with five students and one classroom. Today there are 2,000 Pivot Point Member Schools and Advanced Training Centers in 73 countries.

Award-winning Founder of Pivot Point International, Leo Passage's name has become synonymous with innovative hair design. Starting his school with five students and one classroom in 1962, he has created the international dynasty that became Pivot Point, using his "scientific approach", a theory that blends and applies artistic and scientific principles to hair.

Leo Passage believes that it all begins in the mind. Whether creating a hair design, sculpture, painting or a company, nothing happens until someone thinks of it.

His own vision for his life's work - and of the creation of Pivot Point - came when he discovered The Bauhaus, the most celebrated art school of modern times. Its aim, as is his, was to train crafts people to elevate their skills to a higher level of artistic creativity.

By adapting the Bauhaus philosophy to the craft of Cosmetology, Pivot Point provides the educational structure to develop true hair designers. Their designers analyze, envision and plan their work. At Pivot Point they believe in the importance of teaching a hair design why as well as how something works. Knowing how only results in technical skills. Knowing why allows the freedom to create. This freedom is achieved through a unique educational delivery system, incorporating interactive technology, the cutting edge of education.

For over 40 years, Pivot Point has created successful careers for thousands of designers - designers who create in the realm of hair design, esthetics and nails, who satisfy millions of clients in salons throughout the world. Many of the principles of art and form and color are used in all three areas of study and practice.

Leo Passage, Founder, Pivot Point International, Inc. often quotes the following:

> *"An artist needs inner confidence and self control and yet must dwell within a real world and be conscious of its interests and requirements".*
> **Johannes Itten (1889-1967)**

History of
Pivot Point International
Founded by Leo Passage

In the '60s...

In 1962 Leo Passage introduced the first Pivot Point curriculums for undergraduate and graduate hair design training. In 1964 the principles of both art and science was published as a textbook, Entr'ee To Hair Design. Because of its tremendous success, a second edition was published and renamed Scientific Approach to Hair Design.

This course and other Pivot Point programs would continuously be updated and improved through the years. By 1965 other schools wanted to use Pivot Point's unique teaching methods and support materials. To fulfill their requests, audiovisual and teacher support materials were produced to back up the program. This was the start of Pivot Point's member school system.

The Late '60s & Early '70s

During the late '60s and early '70s, Leo successfully introduced his Pivot Point programs to schools and graduate centers throughput the United States, Canada, Scandinavia, Japan and Australia. Because of the expansion into foreign countries, Pivot Point began translating the programs into various languages.

During this period Leo began manufacturing tools and hair goods for the industry in order to better teach Pivot Point's concepts. Unique items, such as the cone-shaped roller, the slip-on and the hair component system, were Pivot Point inventions. At first, Pivot Point imported European mannequins to the United States for its undergraduate and graduate courses. Over time, economic demand required mannequin production to relocate to Hong Kong to accommodate school market orders. With an uncompromising standard for high-quality mannequins, Pivot Point became fully involved with the creation and manufacturing process. The first objective - which would become the hallmark for Pivot Point mannequins for the next 40+ years - was to create a mannequin that reflected the Pivot Point Difference. A strongly focused approach to the hair implantation process, resulted in life-like, natural hair-growth direction at different angles, closely resembling a live model.

The Late '70s

In 1976, Pivot Point took yet another step to unite the hair and beauty industry by hosting the World Forum in Chicago. Twenty-five countries from around the world participated, and the World Forum grew into a biennial event called the International Teacher's Symposium.

Over the years, the Symposium has become more directed, offering teachers' training courses and business seminars for school administrators. And, in 1991 Pivot Point expanded its Symposium audience to include the salon market as well.

Holland, South Africa and parts of South America were introduced to the Pivot Point method. In 1979, Leo Passage received permission to enter China. Since no Western hair designer had been admitted into China since the revolution, Leo Passage and his International Artistic Team became part of history-making exchange program.

Meanwhile educators back at World Headquarters were busy creating and updating curriculums. One at a time the original step-by-step programs were adjusted to meet Pivot Point's rigorous scientific standards. Current programs include: Scientific Approach to Hair Sculpture/Ladies and Men, Scientific Approach of Hair Design (three volumes: Design Classics, Design System and Long Hair Design) Scientific Approach to Perm, and Scientific Approach to Color.

The '80s

During the 1980s, salon needs were answered with what is now internationally known as Design Forum. This continuing education course, which actually debuted in 1965, has been published over the years as Tomorrow's Creation, Style of the Month, Hair

Fashion of the Month, Aura, Continuing Education Course (CEC), and finally the current Design Forum.

Throughout the years Pivot Point remained involved in competition by conducting workshops taught by world champion designers. It was Pivot Point's belief that competition provided young designers with a necessary means of showing off their talents.

In response to professional demand, Pivot Point began to research and develop a program to help designers better understand and deal with that all-important element of the hair and beauty business (and everyday life) - people skills. Three years in the making, Pivot Point's unique People Skills Program was introduced in 1988. This program exemplifies the fact that, as industry research point out, as much as 80% of a designer's success depends on his or her ability to deal effectively with clients, co-workers and supervisors. Only 20% is due to the designer's technical ability!

Because of the widespread success of this program, other service industries, such as the hospitality industry in New Zealand, requested that Pivot Point tailor the People Skills program to reflect their particular needs. So, in response to this need, representatives of the Polytechnic system of New Zealand adapted People Skills to their Hospitality-related programs.

The '90s

It was at the World Championships in 1990 that Pivot Point first introduced Level 1 and Level 3 multi-media laserdisc programming at an education forum sponsored by the Dutch Hairdresser's Organization. In 1991 Pivot Point launched their sculpture and perm programs in the new laserdisc format. During this time, Leo Passage and his team test-marketed this new multi-media interactive programming throughout the Pivot Point member school network with an overwhelmingly positive response.

The '00s

With the new century in full gear and new technology such as DVD and CD-ROM, Pivot Point believes that students will enjoy a great educational experience with higher retention and better understanding of the concepts and techniques presented. Pivot Point looks forward to a future filled with educational advancement and success. As the company continues to grow, Pivot Point will keep exploring new territories and new ways to bring superior education to the exciting, ever-changing hair and beauty industry.

'67 INTERNATIONAL BEAUTY SHOW
NEW YORK HILTON
NEW YORK CITY
MARCH 13-14-15, 1967

1967 International Beauty Show
New York Hilton, New York City
March 1967

Courtesy of Pivot Point International

Competition

World Championships • World Olympics of Hairstyling • OMC HairWorld and the World Championships of Beauty • Organisation Mondiale Coiffure National Cosmetology Association and The International Beauty Show

Inside the beauty industry exists an exciting arena of artistic and competitive events that culminate in international competitions where competitors, trainers and countries vie for the ultimate title of "World Champion". These events are now known as OMC HairWorld Championships of Beauty and are hosted every two years by the Organisation Mondiale Coiffure, which has 500,000 members in 65 countries and has been conducting international competitions for 60 years. You can visit their web site at www.omchairworld.com to see pictures of the styles and models of the recent competitions. These competitions were last held in Chicago, IL (USA) in 2008 and will be held again in 2010 in Paris, France. This worldwide organization is committed to education and excellence at the highest level. The international competitions and contacts available through membership, promote the sharing of ideas, competence and experiences to promote hairdressing at its highest level and the transfer of this excellence to daily salon life.

"Nize" competes in this international arena with all the pageantry, drama and intensity of the "Olympic" sports events – international flags flying; foreign languages being spoken through cheers, tears and shouts of pure joy. Shining trophies are awarded at the Final Ceremony with pomp and circumstance. The individual and team winners leave with their lives changed forever much like the story of "Nize".

Prior to 1962, the US and the National Cosmetology Association did not participate officially in what was then known as "The Olympics" held by OMC. Up until that time, several different venues existed for international competitions. One was the International Beauty Show, held annually in New York. The other, was held by the OMC, every two years, in different countries. Beginning in 1962, the US and the National Cosmetology Association began sending US teams to OMC World Championship competitions.

The International Beauty Show has become one of the worlds largest trade shows, with over 50,000 attendees. It is still held every year in New York City.

The National Cosmetology Association (NCA) was founded in 1921 and represents the interests of the professional salon industry in the USA. Today, NCA's membership includes more than 25,000 salon owners, hairdressers, nail technicians, estheticians, educators, and students - and is the largest association of salon professionals in the USA. They are USA affiliate members of OMC.

OMC is the producer of OMC HairWorld and The World Championship of Beauty competitions (the "Olympics" of hair).

The author of "Nize", Esther, as Trainer, and her students, participated in the International Beauty Show in New York in 1968 and 1969 where they placed first in the World's Supreme Student Hair-Styling Competition against other students and trainers from around the world.

Included in this section of the book are pictures from the 2008 Chicago HairWorld competitions that give the reader an insight into these events. Further information on the current OMC World Championships and the Organisation Mondiale Coiffure can be obtained at **www.omchairworld.com**. Further information on the International Beauty Show can be found at **www.ibsnewyork.com**. Further information on the National Cosmetology Association can be found at **www.ncacares.org**.

Some of the Winners from the 2008 World Championships

OMC HairWorld
Championships of Beauty 2008 – Chicago, IL

2008 OMC HairWor

Award Ceremonies

Acknowledgements

I humbly acknowledge that all works, such as writing and producing a book like, "Nize", require the contribution of countless individuals and their network of support. This was certainly true with this book which has been in progress, in one way or another, all my life. I did not ever expect to write a book in my early years but all my experiences, family, friends, peers, students, teachers and customers were my inspiration and support beyond my greatest expectation. I do not want to exclude any and therefore have not tried to list everyone who has meant so much to me over the years. This book was the best way I could try to show my gratitude and love for everyone who has helped me.

I do need to give special thanks to my first editor, Jeff Crawford, and his wonderful mother, "Mrs. Crawford".

Daniel Norris, Editor and Publisher, you were a "Godsend" and it was your creative talent and energy that made this book a reality. I am proud to be in your portfolio of publications. Finding you is like the story "Acres of Diamonds".

Leo Passage, Pivot Point International, Inc, and Mia Kim at Pivot Point (special thanks Mia), B. R. Mitchell, Charles Troutman, "Red" Harrisson, Doyle Sherrill, Mazie Frink, Lucy Collier, Dr. Joe Carter, Christine Hewette, Computer Concepts, The Shipping Station, Brunswick Office Supply, National Cosmetology Association, Organization Moindale Coiffure, National Cosmetology Association of North Carolina, Connie Babson, Reita Cockrell, Ashley Talley, Carolina Beach's Island Gazette, Southport-Fort Fisher Ferry personnel, Lois and others at the Rourk Branch, Brunswick County Library are just a few of my many helpers, friends and special teachers who helped me along the way.

My special love to my son Willard and his wonderful family, my daughter-in-law, Beverly, and my grand-daughters, Lindsay and Paige, you are the light of my life and I love you forever. Son, you may recognize some of this but check your birth certificate and my marriage certificate and you will know this is a work of Fiction, despite some familiar stories.

My "helpmate" and husband "Jeff" who I truly love and who never wavered once from my request, on our "Honeymoon", 22 years ago, to help me write a "book". God knew what he was doing when He brought us together.

My step-daughters, Dandridge and Michaux and Michaux's husband Richard and my step-grandchildren Noah, Micah and Hannah. I love each of you.

My brother, Kenneth, who did drive a little red cart pulled by "Billy" and my nephew, Dwight, who has been a "rock' in our family though many difficult times. I love you both.

My parents, Anson and Hillery. They were "the wind beneath my wings".

To the contestants and their lovely models – my congratulations and "thank you so much."

And always and for as long as I live I give all the credit to God, my Friend and Protector.

Credits

March 30, 2008

p. 86, 162, 167
Photos courtesy of Pivot Point International, Inc.

p. 2, 24, 26-27, 28, 96, 152, 156
Daniel Ray Norris

p. 158, 159, 160, 161, 169, 170, 171, 172-173
Esther Myles personal collection

cover, back, p. 5, 6, 10, 14, 16, 20, 28, 32, 36, 40, 42, 46, 51, 52, 58, 62, 66, 70, 74, 78, 82, 92, 100, 104, 110, 114, 118, 122, 126, 130, 134, 138, 142, 146, 154-155
iStockphoto.com

p. 160 (certificate, ground breaking)
The Brunswick Beacon

Dear Esther,

It is with pleasure that I support your book, which will be an inspiration for the young talented hairdressers to become champions in their everyday lives and ultimate OMC World Champions.

Best of luck,

Salvatore Fodera

Salvatore Fodera
OMC World President

Salvatore Fodera, OMC World President

The Family
Married to Mary, 2 sons
Gianni - Hairstylist / World Champion
Vincent - Hairstylist

The Entrepreneur
Owner of Salon Fodera at 5-star hotel St. Regis in New York City

The Honoree
NCA Member
NCA Hall of Fame
NCA Pillar in Leadership

The Competitor
Team and Individual OMC World Champion
Won all major national and international prizes:
Europe Cup / Rose d'Or / Golden Tulip

The World President of OMC
President of the World Hairdressers' Organization (OMC) since 2004
Instrumental in restructuring OMC:
Updated and developed competitions world-wide
Introduced Fashion and Technical categories with distinct World Cups
Created educational & training programs world-wide
Founder and President of the OMC Prestige Club